I struggled for a moment with my conscience. I would have liked to hold Keri responsible, but I knew, really and truly, that I could only blame myself. I had gone out with another boy, just to see if another boy would be more exciting. OK, so Keri was the one who had egged me on, but that only meant I was pathetic and weak-willed and had no mind of my own.

"Would you go back with Rees," said Frizz, "if he asked you?"

"He won't."

"No, but if he did?"

"I told you, he won't!" Why would he ever even want to see me again, let alone go out with me?

Girlfriends

Also by Jean Ure
in the Girlfriends series

Girls Stick Together!

Girls Are Groovy!

Pink Knickers Aren't Cool!

Boys Are OK!

Boys R Us

Boys Will Be Boys

Boys Behaving Badly

Orchard Black Apples

Get a Life

Just Sixteen

Love is for Ever

ORCHARD BOOKS
338 Euston Road, London NW1 3BH
Orchard Books Australia
Level 17/207 Kent Street, Sydney, NSW 2000

First published in 2010 by Orchard Books

ISBN 978 1 40830 304 7

Text © Jean Ure 2010

1 3 5 7 9 10 8 6 4 2
Printed in Great Britain

Orchard Books is a division of Hachette Children's Books,
an Hachette UK company.

www.hachette.co.uk

Boys Are Back

JEAN URE

ORCHARD BOOKS

Chapter 1

"Me and Rees have broken up."

That's what I would say. All cool and casual, like so what? Who cares? Not me!

I practised it, pacing to and fro across my bedroom. *Me and Rees have broken up.* No big deal. We've broken up! OK? I waved a hand. The hand waved back at me, from my dressing table mirror. Omigod, I looked like totally demented! My hair was standing on end where I'd raked my fingers through it, and my glasses had slipped to the end of my nose and were about to fall off. Savagely, I thrust them back and snatched up a hair brush to beat my hair. I was going round to Keri's in a minute. Dad was giving me a lift. We were all going to be there, me and Keri, Lily and Frizz. I desperately didn't want them to feel sorry for me!

I suddenly felt my legs were about to give way, and had to sink down onto my bed. I was all trembly, like a jelly. Five minutes ago I'd been happily looking forward to meeting up with the others and telling them all the latest news, like how me and Rees were going back to our dog training classes. How I'd promised Rees faithfully that I would try really hard not to let him down. Last time, Bundle had behaved just *so* badly. I hadn't ever wanted to go back. It had been too humiliating, having a dog who just galloped about grinning and barking, refusing to be trained. But I felt I owed it to Rees cos I'd been behaving just as badly as Bundle, going out with that horrible Rory behind Rees's back. Rees had wanted me to go with him. I'd explained to him why I couldn't. I'd told him that I was very sorry but I'd promised Keri I would go somewhere with her. I hadn't mentioned the actual place, and I hadn't mentioned Rory. But I *had* said sorry and Rees had accepted it. At least, I thought he had.

"Polly?" he said; and I'd known at once that something was wrong. Just the way he said it. *Polly*. Like cold, and accusing. "I've cancelled this afternoon."

I said, "C-cancelled? Our dog class?"

"Yes."

"But why?"

"I think you know why," said Rees.

I protested that I didn't, but horrid clammy fingers were already creeping up my spine. "If it's about last Saturday... I told you! It was something I couldn't get out of. I'm really, really sorry!"

"So'm I," said Rees. "Still, at least it means you won't have to be embarrassed again. I know you didn't really want to go on with the classes."

"I did!" I cried. "I did! I want Bundle to be trained!"

"That's OK," said Rees. "You'll find someone else to go with."

"I don't want to go with anyone else."

"Should have thought of that before," said Rees.

That was when I knew for sure: he'd found out about Rory. Someone must have told him! But who? There was only one person I could think of, and that was Craig. He's my brother, and you would suppose he might be at least a *little* bit loyal; but sometimes I think boys can be just as mean and spiteful as girls are said to be. It isn't even true about girls! Only some are like that. Frizz isn't; neither is Lily. Even Keri, for all her big mouth, wouldn't go telling tales behind my back. Why on earth should she? One thing's for sure, you certainly wouldn't expect it of *your own brother*. But Craig goes to the same school as Rees, they are even in the same class, and it just seemed like too much of a coincidence.

Dad's voice called up at me from the garden: "Polly! You ready?"

I had to go; I had to be brave. As I reached the head of the stairs I bumped into Craig, on his way up.

"Well, thank you very much!" I snarled.

"For what?" said Craig.

"For telling Rees about last Saturday!"

Craig tossed his head. "*I* didn't tell him."

"Don't lie!"

"I'm not lying, you pile of horse droppings!"

I looked at him through narrowed eyes. "So if you didn't," I said, "who did?"

"Don't ask me! I don't go round tattling." He shoved rudely past me. I grabbed the banister rail just in time. That boy has *no* manners. "Mind you," he yelled, as he stomped off to his bedroom, "it's no more than you deserve!"

It *was* him. It had to be! Except…tiny tendrils of doubt were beginning to snake their way in. Craig is like just about the most totally annoying person in the entire universe, but he is usually quite truthful. He is more likely to boast about the things he has done, rather than deny them. On the other hand…*who else could it be*?

I didn't have time to stop and ponder. Dad was shouting at me that he would be late if I didn't get a move on. I had to go and face the others.

"Me and Rees have broken up."

I said it just like I'd planned. Careless. Casual. So what? I waited to see who would react first. Keri, of course! It's always Keri.

"What happened?" she said.

I took a deep breath. "He found out. About Saturday."

"But I thought you'd already got it sorted?" That was

Lily, plainly puzzled. "We had it all out!"

"Had what out?" said Frizz.

"Well…" Lily hesitated, obviously not sure how much I would want them to know. The fact was, I'd rung her up in a state cos of Rory trying to do things I didn't want him to do. He'd tried to kiss me! A full, slobbery sort of kiss, all wet and slurpy. I didn't feel ready for that! It had really upset me. But Lily had been such a good friend. She'd met me in the shopping centre and tried to calm me down as I told her all about it. How I'd got in a panic and pretended to have come out without my epi pen (which is this thing I need cos of being allergic to insect bites) so that I'd have an excuse for running home and leaving Rory on his own with Keri and her boyfriend Dermot.

"*What* did you have out?" demanded Keri.

"Oh! Just…about Rees," said Lily, "and what she ought to do. I told her to ring him up and apologise, and that's what you were doing. *Wasn't* it?" She turned to me, and I nodded miserably. "She was on the phone, talking to him, when I left. I thought it was all going OK?"

I said, "It was. It did! But somehow he's found out about me going to Hadleigh House, and—"

"You mean you didn't *tell* him?" said Frizz.

"No!" My voice came out in a thin wail.

"I suppose that means you didn't tell him about Rory, either?"

"God," said Keri, "she wouldn't want to do that!"

11

"What did you actually say to him?" said Frizz, sounding rather stern.

I hiccuped. "I just s-said...I'd g-gone somewhere with Keri that I'd arranged ages ago and couldn't get out of it."

There was a silence.

"That sounds like really convincing," said Keri.

"Well, I said it a bit better than that! I said I was really sorry. Which I was! And Rees said that was all right, he wasn't mad or anything. I told him I'd go back to dog training classes, we were going to go this afternoon, and then he suddenly rang up all cold and said he'd cancelled."

"Did he say why?"

"No, but I know why. Somebody obviously told him."

Keri leaned forward. "Who d'you think it could be?"

"I don't know. I thought it was Craig, but he says it wasn't."

"Well, it wasn't me," said Lily.

"Nor me," said Frizz.

"I know it wasn't you!"

"It's got to be Craig,"

"But he swears it wasn't!"

"Actually," Keri cleared her throat. For once in her life, she actually looked embarrassed. "It might have been me."

Keri?

We all turned to stare. Two spots of pink had appeared in her cheeks. It was the first time I had ever,

12

ever seen Keri blush. Quickly she said, "I didn't do it on purpose! I'm not a snitch. But Mum asked me whether we'd had a good time, and I said yes, except that you'd had to go home because of forgetting your pen thing, which meant poor old Rory being left like the odd one out. You know? And then—" She swallowed, and the spots of pink grew brighter and more hectic. "This morning," mumbled Keri, "I went into town with Mum, and we bumped into Rees's mum, cos like my mum and Rees's mum know each other?"

I knew that. I nodded anxiously. "Just get on with it."

"Yeah, well, Rees's mum was going on about this wasps' nest they'd got in their garden? How they were going to have to get it removed? And my mum said wasps could be dangerous if you happened to be allergic, and Rees's mum said yes, like Polly, and—"

I gritted my teeth.

"Well, anyway, Mum just happened to mention how we'd all gone to Hadleigh House and how you'd left your pen thing behind and had to go home and what a shame it was, and—" Keri gave a little embarrassed laugh. "How two's company, three's a crowd, kind of thing?"

"You mean, she told her about Rory?"

"She didn't *tell* her, she just *mentioned* it. In passing. She didn't know you were going out with him behind Rees's back. She probably didn't even know you'd ever gone out with Rees in the first place!"

"I would have thought," said Lily, "you could have found some way of stopping her."

"Like how?"

"I don't know! Suddenly passing out, or something."

"In the middle of the shopping centre?"

"I would have!"

"Look, I'm *sorry*," said Keri, "but it wasn't my fault. These things happen. If you will try to go out with two boys at the same time—"

"You were the one that egged her on," said Frizz.

"She didn't need egging on! She'd already practically decided to give Rees the elbow."

That was so not true! I hadn't!

"But you had, you know," said Frizz, as she and I wandered back together afterwards, down the hill to the bus stop. "You told me yourself…that time you wanted me to lie for you? Say you were with me when you were going out with that boy that was a friend of Keri's boyfriend?"

"Rory," I muttered. It was the same boy. The one that had tried to slobber over me. Ugh! How could I ever have fancied him?

"You said you were too young to be tied to one person."

"I didn't mean I wanted to stop seeing Rees!"

"No, you meant you wanted to try going out with

14

other boys and see if you liked them better than you liked him. Admit it!" said Frizz.

I sighed. There was some truth in what she was saying. OK! More than just some truth. Rees was the only boy I'd ever been out with. I needed to know what other boys were like. It wasn't so much that I was bored with Rees, just that he wasn't very…romantic. I wanted the tingle factor! I wanted excitement! What I didn't want was great wet slobby kisses before I felt ready for them.

I said this to Frizz and she shrugged and said, "Chance you take when you go on a blind date."

I was indignant. It wasn't a blind date! Well…maybe it was. Strictly speaking. But so what?

"You might be a bit more sympathetic," I grumbled. "You are supposed to be my friend… My *oldest* friend. Just cos you and Darren are like stuck together with superglue—"

I stopped, before I could say something I might regret. We sometimes used to laugh, just a little bit, at Frizz and Darren. Keri always said they were like some ancient married couple, doddering about together.

Frizz was looking at me. She said, "What about me and Darren?"

"Well, it's just…you know! You're happy together. You don't want anyone else! We can't all be that lucky. Some of us have to go out with loads of different boys before we find the right one."

Frizz curled her lip. "Like Keri, you mean."

"*Not* like Keri." Keri changed boyfriends practically every week. "I would hate to be like that!" Fat chance, even if I'd wanted. Keri seems to have some sort of magnetism where the opposite sex is concerned. Of course she is very tall and slim and bursting with confidence, whereas I am short and somewhat on the dumpy side, and wear glasses, and have next to no confidence at all.

"But the first boy you go out with," I insisted, "isn't necessarily the *right* boy. Not for most people. That's all I'm saying."

"Yes, and I quite understand," said Frizz. "I didn't see anything wrong in you going out with this Rory person. I just thought it was wrong to go out with him while you were still seeing Rees."

I couldn't argue with that. I'd known I was behaving badly, even at the time. "But I still think it was mean of Keri to go and tell her mum!"

"She didn't know her mum was going to bump into Rees's mum."

"But she knows they know each other!"

"She didn't know Rees's mum was going to start talking about wasps' nests."

But like Lily had said, she could have fainted, or something. Created some kind of diversion. That was what a true friend would have done.

"Be fair," said Frizz.

I clenched my fists into tight balls. I felt like screaming, "Don't keep making excuses for her!" All I wanted was a little friendly support and understanding and all I was getting was some kind of lecture.

"She did say she was sorry."

"She didn't sound very sorry!"

"That's probably cos she's feeling guilty."

I said, "*Keri?*"

"Well, she was the one that set it all up."

At last! I agreed, eagerly, that if it hadn't been for Keri, I would never have gone out with another boy in the first place. "It was entirely her fault!"

"Not entirely," said Frizz. "After all, you didn't *have* to go."

Really, it was just as well that at that point my bus came and I was able to jump on it and leave Frizz behind. She was definitely starting to get on my nerves. As for Keri feeling guilty...forget it!

Craig was on his way out as I arrived home. He hissed, "Listen, you! I'm sick of always being accused of doing things I haven't done. I wasn't the one that shopped you!"

I pushed past him. "I know you weren't."

"Oh! So you know, do you? So am I going to get an apology?"

I shouted, "I apologise!" and slammed the back gate behind me.

"Are you two fighting again?" said Mum.

I said, "No, it's just something I thought he'd done."

"And he hadn't?"

Mum raised an eyebrow, inviting confidences, but I pretended not to notice. Me and Mum have this really great relationship, we discuss loads of girly stuff together, the sort of stuff I couldn't possibly talk to Dad about. Not that Dad doesn't try his best to be helpful, it's just that being a man he doesn't always understand. But this was something I couldn't bring myself to confess, even to Mum. I guess I was just too ashamed…

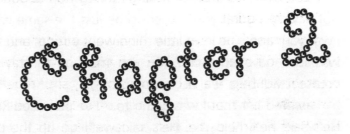

Chapter 2

Unfortunately, I'd already made a big thing of announcing how me and Rees were going back to dog training classes. Earlier in the week, Craig had brought Bundle back from his walk covered all over in stinky fox poo. I had gone, "Yeeurgh! That's disgusting! How could you let him do it?" Which was actually unfair, cos he'd once done it with me. It is one of his doggy delights, to find a pile of poo and roll in it.

"Couldn't you have stopped him?" wailed Mum.

Craig said, "How? He doesn't take any damn notice. Just sees a mess and dives straight in. Might as well talk to a brick wall."

That was when I had made my announcement. "Don't worry, I'm taking him back to classes. And this time," I vowed, "he's going to do as he's told!"

"Way to go," Mum had said, rather grimly pulling on a pair of rubber gloves.

She'd told me later that she was glad I'd decided to try

again. She said it showed persistence.

"You do have a bit of a tendency to hop about. I'm not having a go at you! I used to be just the same when I was your age. The least little thing went wrong, and that was it...I gave up. So if you can manage to stay the course it will be a real achievement."

I assured her that I was going to. "I've promised Rees. He's said he'll help me. He's said we'll go up the park every single day next week and practise."

Next week was half term, and now I was going to be at a total loose end. Nowhere to go, nothing to do, no one to see. But before that there was this Saturday afternoon to get through. I was going to have to think of something to tell Mum. She was still expecting me to take Bundle to his dog training class.

"What time are you off?" she said. "Two o'clock?"

Craig shot me a look. We were in the kitchen, eating lunch. That is, me and Mum and Craig. Dad was still at work. I was glad Dad wasn't there. It was going to be bad enough explaining to Mum.

"Do you want a lift?" she said. "Or is Rees picking you up?"

There was a pause.

"Ahem," said Craig.

Like anybody ever says *ahem*! I kicked at him under the table.

"Pol?"

I swallowed hard on a mouthful of cheese roll. In this loud, trumpeting voice I said, "Me and Rees have broken up."

"Oh, Polly!" Mum turned swiftly, with a look of real concern. "I'm so sorry! When did that happen?"

I mumbled, "Just this morning."

"This morning?"

Like I was bothered? I stuffed my mouth with more cheese roll and chomped defiantly.

"Did you quarrel, or what?" said Mum.

Craig made a vulgar scoffing noise. "Boys don't quarrel! They leave that sort of thing to girls."

I said, "Yes, boys just *fight*." A blodge of cheese shot out of my mouth and landed on the back of Craig's hand.

"Bloody hell!" roared Craig.

"Boys punch each other. *Far* more civilised."

"I'll punch you," said Craig, "if you're not careful!" He picked off the cheese and flicked it back at me.

"Oh, God," said Mum.

"Horse droppings!"

"Fox poo!"

"Button it!" Mum rapped crossly on the table with a spoon. "And you, Bundle, get down! We're not having dogs on the table. I presume," she added, rather bitterly, "that's the end of obedience training?"

I shrugged. "Might be. Dunno yet. Might go with someone else."

"Who'd wanna go with you?" jeered Craig.

"Craig," said Mum, "I'm warning you…"

I was really hoping that would be the end of it, cos I really *really* didn't want to have to talk about me and Rees, not even to Mum, but sometimes I think Mum can read my mind. It's like she gets in there and knows exactly what I'm feeling. At least she waited till Craig had taken himself off. You can't have a sensible conversation with him around. Not that I was going to have a conversation. Not if I could help it.

"You're sounding very upbeat," said Mum. "I'm glad you're taking it so calmly."

I gave a little sickly smile and said, "I guess that's life."

"I guess it is," said Mum. And then, as I tried to slide out through the door: "Are you really taking it calmly?"

I did my best to turn the sickly smile into a dazzling beam. "Sure thing," I said. "I'm far too young to have a permanent boyfriend."

"True." Mum nodded slowly. "But I always thought you and Rees were such good pals. Not just boyfriend and girlfriend, but real chums."

Who wanted to be *chums*? It wasn't what it was about! I said this to Mum and she frowned.

"Your dad and I are chums."

I thought yes, that was because they'd been together for ages. They'd probably lost the tingle factor years ago. I said, "I bet you weren't chums when you started off."

22

"Well, not immediately," said Mum, "but by the time we got married—"

"You were *chums*?"

"Of course we were!"

"But what about the romance?"

Mum smiled. "You're telling me you didn't have any with Rees?"

"I was getting kind of bored," I said. I hated myself even as I said it. But Mum had pushed me into it! I wasn't the one who'd wanted to talk. Greatly daring I added, "He didn't have any tingle factor."

"Right. OK! I hear you. I still think it's a shame," said Mum. "He's such a nice boy. I never used to worry when you were with him."

"Well, this is it," I said.

"What's that supposed to mean? *This is it*?"

"You didn't have anything to worry about!"

"So?"

"Well—" I waved a hand. Did I really have to explain?

"You *want* me to worry?" said Mum. "You'd actually like it if I sat at home chewing my nails and wondering what you were getting up to?"

I said, "N-no. Not exactly. Just – well!"

"Well?"

Earnestly I told her that I wouldn't ever actually *get up* to anything.

"But you'd like there to be the possibility?"

I hung my head. It sounded kind of gross, put like that.

"Oh, get away with you!" said Mum. She made shooing motions in the direction of the back door. "If you're not taking that dog to obedience classes, at least take him for a run – and *don't let him roll in anything!*"

It was my turn to take Bundle out, so I couldn't really argue. As we walked up the road – Bundle on the lead, doing his usual tug-tug, pant-tug – I wondered if I really did want there to be the possibility. I came to the conclusion that I did. I did! Only it had to be the right person; not just anybody. I still cringed at the thought of Rory and his big blobby lips coming towards me. I sort of cringed at the thought of any lips coming towards me. I just didn't get the kissing thing. Someone's tongue in your mouth! Yuck! But then, if it were the right person...

We reached the park and I let Bundle off the lead. He went bounding off at once towards a couple of Jack Russells that were playing with a ball. I love how dogs can just go up to other dogs and join in their games. It never crosses their minds that they might not be wanted. They don't have to bother with introductions, or wait to be asked. It's just, like, "Hi, there! I've come to play".

I watched for a moment as the three of them went streaming across the grass together, then wandered on down the path, thinking of lips and tongues and trying to attach them to the right person. What sort of person would the right person be? Divinely attractive; that went without saying. Black hair, very thick and glossy. Deep brown eyes. Beautiful smile. Straight nose. Athletic-looking, but not mad and sporty. I wouldn't want anyone that was a football freak. Maybe a swimmer. That would be nice, cos then I could imagine him in swimming trunks, all tanned and glistening, diving off the top board. Oh, and he'd be tall, of course. Well, tall*ish*. Not hugely so, cos then he'd tower over me and that would look stupid. Just tall enough not to be short.

It occurred to me that I already knew this divinely attractive boy. It was Joel, who was Lily's partner at dancing school. I blushed at the thought. I could never tell Lily! And anyway, it was all completely futile. Joel was gay, and even if he hadn't been he'd never look twice at someone like me. He hadn't even looked twice at Lily. Not in that way. And Lily is the daintiest and prettiest of us all! She and Joel were good friends, but even Lily had come to accept that that was all they would ever be. She had spent months sighing over Joel. Keri had always told her she was wasting her time, but you can't just turn your emotions on and off at will. Not if your feelings for someone are really honest and true.

I had just embarked on a pleasant daydream where Joel and me, by some miracle, were going out together, when I heard a shout of, "Scuse me! Your dog's got our ball!" I looked up to see Bundle joyously galloping towards me, pursued by two maddened Jack Russells.

Bundle had something red and squishy clamped between his teeth. Somehow or other, he was managing to grin at the same time. My heart sank. Getting a ball away from him is next to impossible.

"Bundle!" I bellowed. "DROP!"

I might as well not have bothered for all the notice he took. He was off and away, wheeling across the park. The only ones that could get anywhere near him were the Jack Russells, but instead of co-operating with each other they broke off to start squabbling. It took me and their owner almost five minutes to coax Bundle into dropping the ball, and we might never have done it at all if a man walking past with a Labrador hadn't stopped to offer a dog biscuit.

"I'm really sorry," I said, handing back a half-chewed ball.

The Jack Russells' owner simply said that dogs would be dogs, but the Labrador man looked at Bundle like he was some kind of juvenile delinquent and told me that I really ought to have more control.

"You need to take that dog to obedience classes."

I went on my way feeling cross and defiant. Dogs would be dogs! Bundle hadn't meant to steal; he just thought it was all part of the game. But I told him to behave himself, and he wagged his tail and looked at me like he was sorry, so I let him off the lead and tried to pick up my daydream again. Joel and me going out together… Joel taking my hand. Putting his arm round me. Drawing me close. *Kissing.* How would it feel? If it were Joel? Would I—

Omigod! "Bundle," I shrieked, "get out of there!"

But I was too late. He'd already done it: covered himself in fox poo. *Again.*

"Well, that's it," said Mum, when we got back home. She pointed. "Rubber gloves. Your turn."

"You are a filthy, repulsive animal," I told Bundle, as I dragged him into the garden.

By the time I'd got him clean, my beautiful daydream had faded. I went upstairs and lay on my bed with my eyes squeezed tight shut, hoping I'd be able to pick up where I'd left off, but try as I might my mind stayed blank. I kept thinking, this is silly! You know perfectly well you're never going to go out with Joel. Even daydreams, I find, have to have a bit of basis in reality. OK to imagine someone *like* Joel; but not *actually* Joel. Except I couldn't even do that. Stinking fox poo had broken the mood.

I thought vengefully that if that stupid Keri hadn't gone and blabbered things out to her mum I'd have been at dog training class with Rees, and Bundle would never have got the chance to roll in poo. But then that would mean me and Rees were still together, and I'd already told Mum I didn't want us to be together. Which I didn't! *Watch my lips.* I mouthed it at myself in the mirror. Just because I couldn't have Joel didn't mean I had to be stuck with Rees. There had to be *someone* more exciting out there!

On impulse, I snatched up my phone and speed dialled the first number that came to me.

"Chloe!" I shrieked. Chloe is like my very best friend at school. I can talk to her as easily as I can to Frizz or Lily. "Chloe, this is Polly!"

Chloe said, "I know it is. Why are you yelling?"

"I'm not yelling."

"Yes, you are. You're nearly blasting my eardrums out."

"Oh. Well. OK." I hadn't realised I was being loud. I'm quite quiet, as a rule. Quite a restrained sort of person, except when Craig is getting on my nerves.

"All up-front and aggressive," grumbled Chloe. "What's the matter with you?"

I said, "Nothing's the matter. I just wanted to tell you, ME AND REES HAVE SPLIT UP."

"Ouch! You're doing it again!"

"Sorry," I said, "sorry, I just wanted you to know that me and Rees have split up." I said it quite calmly; I didn't shout. "We're not seeing each other any more."

There was a moment of silence, then Chloe said, "So are you OK with it?"

"Me? I'm fine. Can't go out with the same person for ever, can you?"

A sort of snorting sound came down the telephone.

"Some of us," said Chloe, "don't get to go out with anyone at all."

"What happened to that Chad guy?" I said. "The one you were so keen on?"

Bitterly Chloe said, "He was going to call me, if you remember."

I did remember. Why had I asked? I knew perfectly well he'd let her down.

"Well, never mind! Plenty more fish in the sea," I said.

Chloe snorted. "That is *such* a stupid expression! Anyway, fish stocks are being seriously depleted, in case you hadn't heard."

I thought, yes, and people like Keri didn't help, going round with nets the size of football pitches, catching every boy that moved.

"Hey, I just had an idea," said Chloe. "If you and Rees have really broken up, maybe I could have him?"

I stared, outraged, at the telephone.

"What d'you reckon?" said Chloe.

"Ha ha," I said. "Big joke!" I suddenly felt that Chloe and I had said everything we needed to say, just for the moment. "Gotta go," I said. "See you around!"

"Yeah, whatever," said Chloe.

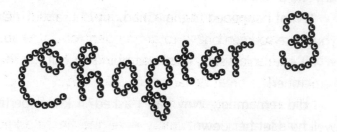

Chapter 3

I was quite surprised on Sunday morning when my phone rang and I saw that it was Keri. I would have thought I'd be the last person she'd want to speak to. Blabbing to her mum like that!

I said, "Keri?" In this rather cold voice, cos I wanted her to know that I was still displeased.

"*Pollee!*" she cried.

It was no use her sounding all bright and chirpy – she wasn't getting round me that easily. *If at all.* As a rule I don't bear grudges, but she'd really gone and done it this time.

"How are you?" she gushed.

I hesitated, wondering whether to be heavily sarcastic, like "Me? I'm over the moon! I've just lost my boyfriend." Or whether I should play it supercool and simply say, "I'm fine, thank you. How are you?"

In the end, I didn't do either. Somewhat tetchily I said,

"What is it? What d'you want?"

"Oh, oh! Pardon me for breathing," said Keri.

"Look, I happen to be in a bit of a rush," I said. "OK?"

"OK, you don't have to get all bent out of shape! It won't take a minute. I just wanted to say that I'm sorry."

Sorry? The great Kerianne Fox was *sorry*?

"I'm apologising, bird brain!"

I swallowed. I don't think, in all the time I'd known her, I had heard Keri apologise. Ever! For anything.

"Honestly, I wouldn't have had it happen for the world! I just never dreamt that Mum would go talking about it to Rees's mum. I mean, it just never occurred to me, you know?"

It wouldn't have occurred to me, either. I tell my mum all sorts of things that I wouldn't want her talking to people about. I began, reluctantly, to feel that perhaps I had been a bit hard on Keri. It wasn't like she had purposely betrayed me.

"It's all right," I said. "Don't worry about it. Wasn't your fault."

"D'you mean that?" She brightened up instantly. "Am I forgiven?"

I struggled a moment; then, a bit grudgingly, said, "I s'pose so."

"I know it was a horrid thing to happen, but it wasn't like Rees was the love of your life, or anything. I mean maybe, in one way, it was just as well... Saved you having

31

to tell him you didn't want to see him any more. Cos that is just *so* awful, when you have to do that. It just makes you feel terrible. And knowing you, you'd probably never have got up the courage, which means you'd still be going out with him and wishing he was someone else. So really," said Keri, "if you look at it that way, I've actually done you a favour! Don't you reckon? When you actually stop and think about it?"

So far, I hadn't really let myself think about it. Not properly. I wasn't sure that I wanted to. I told Keri that just because I'd accepted her apology, it didn't mean she could start getting all cocky.

"No, absolutely not," said Keri. "This is why I'm ringing, cos I feel so guilty. I'm going to make it up to you! You're on half term same as me, right?"

I said, "Right." Maybe not quite as enthusiastically as I could have done. When Keri said she was going to make it up to me...what exactly did she mean by that? After my experience with Rory and his slobbering, I wasn't sure how much I trusted her.

"Fancy coming for a ride?" said Keri. "Horse ride? Tuesday morning, half eleven? Mum and me'll pick you up."

"But I can't ride," I said.

"Doesn't matter! We'll put you on someone nice and quiet and we'll just go for a gentle plod."

Guardedly I said, "You mean, just the two of us?"

"Well, n-no... Jake'll be there. And maybe this other boy? Stuart? He might come."

I was instantly suspicious. "Who's Jake?" I said. "And who's Stuart?"

"Jake's this boy at the stables? He keeps his horse there. I told you about him before."

"What happened to Dermot?" I said.

"Dermot's gone off to America with his mum and dad."

"You mean you're seeing this other boy while he's away?"

"No! What d'you take me for?" Keri sounded indignant. As if she would do such a thing! "His dad's got a job over there. They're not coming back."

"Well, you sound *really* broken up," I said. I couldn't resist it. Keri has had more boyfriends than most people have hot dinners.

"Wasn't like we were soul mates," said Keri. "He was just someone to knock around with." She giggled. "Wait till you've seen Jake!"

"What about this Stuart?"

"He's nice, you'll like him."

"But who is he?"

"Just someone I met at the stables. He doesn't have his own horse or anything. He only started taking lessons a few weeks ago, so you'll be in good company."

I said, "Huh!" Keri's idea of good company wasn't

necessarily the same as mine. "He's not like Rory," I said, "is he?"

"God, no!" Keri went off into peals of laughter. "They couldn't be more different. That's why I said you'll like him. Oh, Polly, come on! You'll enjoy it, I know you will."

I had to admit I was tempted, cos I do love horses. When I was little I'd wanted *so* much to go riding, but Mum had always said we couldn't afford it. Suddenly apprehensive, I said, "How much does it cost?"

"Won't cost anything! It's my treat. I owe it to you. Just say you'll come!"

"Can I ring you back?" I said. "I'll have to check with Mum."

Before I checked with Mum, I had to check with myself. Did I really want to go and meet this Stuart person? Cos I knew that's what it was all about. It wasn't about riding, it was about fixing me up with another boy so she could stop feeling guilty. But did I want to be fixed up with another boy? Specially one chosen by Keri. Suppose it turned out to be disastrous all over again?

I tried calling Lily, who'd been so sweet before, but she wasn't picking up. So then I tried Frizz, who once upon a time would have been my number one choice. We've known each other practically for ever, longer even than I've known the others. It was just that Frizz, lately, or so it seemed to me, had had a tendency to be somewhat picky and judgemental. I didn't want to be lectured! But when I told her I was in a muddle about what to do she sounded sympathetic and said why not come over, so I yelled at Dad that I was going to see Frizz and went zooming up the road to catch a bus.

I thought, *this is like the old days,* as I settled cross-legged on Frizz's bed and prepared for a cosy chat.

"See, I'd just adore to go for a ride," I said, "specially as Keri's going to pay, which I reckon is OK cos a) she owes me and b) she has this whacking great allowance."

Frizz nodded. "Yup! I'd say that was all right."

"She really is trying to make up for what she did."

"So she ought," said Frizz. "She's got away with things for far too long."

"She has," I said. "That's why I don't mind her paying for me."

"So what is it you're in a muddle about?"

I pulled a face. "This boy."

"*Another* boy?"

"Stuart. She says he's just started learning to ride and he's really nice and I'll like him."

Frizz drew in her breath. "Not sure that's such a good idea. Not after last time."

"I know!" I wailed it, pathetically.

"If you want my opinion," said Frizz, "you'll tell her you don't want to meet any more boys."

I looked at her, horrified. "Not ever?"

"Not any she's likely to introduce you to. You know

what sort of crowd she hangs out with."

Rich and spoilt, mostly. I still remembered the ghastly girl she'd once had staying with her. *Mima,* short for Jemima. All loud and shrieky. And she and Keri had laughed at Frizz for being dumb.

"Thing is," I said, "he's not an actual *friend,* I don't think. Just someone she's met at the stables. When I asked her if he was anything like Rory, she laughed and said no, he was quite different."

"Different how?"

"Dunno, she didn't say...but I would just *adore* to go riding!"

"Well, it's up to you," said Frizz.

"I've got to have some kind of social life!"

"Doesn't have to be with Keri. Why not come out with me and Darren?"

I looked at her doubtfully. "You wouldn't want me there," I said.

"Course I would, you're my best friend."

"That is so lovely," I said. "But what would Darren say?"

"Wouldn't say anything! Not if I told him not to."

Frizz still had Darren under her thumb from the time she'd caught him kissing another girl at a party. But I shook my head.

"It wouldn't be fair."

"Tell you what," said Frizz, "Darren's got a mate... Kevin Boon? Why don't we go out as a foursome?"

I was still doubtful, but I promised Frizz I would think about it. I was really touched she would do something like that for me, cos I know how much she and Darren like to be on their own. But oh, I did *so* want to go riding!

"Let me know," said Frizz.

I said, "I will, I will! I'll give you a call."

On my way out I bumped into Darren, who was about to ring at the front door. He said, "Hi, Polly."

I said, "Hi, Darren." Hi is about all we ever do say to each other. We don't have very much in common.

"Just been to see Frizz," I said.

"Dawn," said Darren. "I call her Dawn."

"Well, of course, it is her name," I agreed. "I suppose I ought to call her that, really."

"Don't think she minds."

"Hey!" Frizz's footsteps came clumping down the stairs. "What are you two talking about?"

"Nothing!" I waved a hand. "I'll call you." I thought on my way back I would stop off at the shopping centre and see if I could find a new top in one of the sales. Just *in case* I decided to take Keri up on her offer; I still hadn't come to any decision.

As I stepped off the escalator on the first floor, a familiar voice cried, "Pollee!" and I spun round to see Katie waving at me from across the store. Katie is another of my friends from school. I immediately raced over to her.

"Where's Chantal?" Chantal is Katie's *best* friend; you hardly ever come across one of them without the other.

"In there." Katie flapped a hand in the direction of the changing rooms. "She's been trying things on for the last half hour. 'What d'you think of this? What d'you think of that?' But I don't know why she bothers cos she doesn't listen to a word I say. Come and see if you can talk sense into her."

The cubicle looked like a clothes bomb had hit it. There were clothes draped everywhere.

I said, "How did you manage to smuggle so many in?"

Chantal giggled. "Just kept going out and helping myself. What d'you think of this skirt?"

"Great," I said, at exactly the same time as Katie said, "Puke! It's *yellow*."

"Well, thank *you*," said Chantal. "That's a lot of help, that is." Crossly, she gathered up an armful of clothes and headed back out. "I'm gonna get some more."

"See what I mean?" said Katie. "She just doesn't *listen*. Anyway, what's new?"

"Nothing much," I said. "Oh, I've broken up with Rees." Ultra cool. Ultra casual. "Apart from that..." I shrugged.

"I thought you two were like a permanent item?"

Primly I said, "We're too young for that."

"Yeah, I guess." Katie picked up one of Chantal's discarded skirts and held it against herself. "Yuck! Gross.

Are you going with anyone else?"

"Not yet," I said. "It only just happened. There's this boy Keri wants to fix me up with. Boy at her riding school. She wants me to go for a ride so I can meet him."

"Sounds great."

"Mm. I s'pose. I can't make up my mind."

"Why?" Katie reached out for another skirt. "Hey, I like this one! D'you think it suits me?" She held it against her, wiggling her hips. "What d'you reckon?"

"Looks lovely," I said.

"I think I'll have it! How about you? You getting anything?"

"Might get a top. Just in case I go and meet this boy."

"Why wouldn't you?"

"Oh...I dunno." I couldn't be bothered going into long explanations. "I might not like him."

"Well, you don't have to see him again, do you?" Katie twirled, in front of the mirror. "Go for it," she said. "I would! Play the field."

I looked at her doubtfully. What did she mean, *play the field*?

"Meet as many guys as you can. If one's no good, try another. It's the only way," said Katie. "It's like choosing clothes...you don't just buy the first thing you see. Same with boys."

I nodded. It seemed to make sense.

"Omigod," said Katie, as the curtain swished back to

reveal Chantal, carrying another bunch of skirts. "She's brought half the store with her!"

Chantal giggled. I'm sure if I tried walking into a changing room with armfuls of clothes, someone would stop me. But Chantal has this, like, *glow*. She is so beautiful it almost hurts. I think people just get dazzled.

Still giggling, she began draping skirts all about the cubicle. "Want to try some on?"

I wouldn't have minded except that Chantal is taller and skinnier than me, so it would probably only have been embarrassing and I couldn't have afforded to buy one anyhow, but Katie very firmly said that we had things to do.

"Me and Polly," she announced, "are going to go and look at tops. And this skirt here" – she pointed – "I'm having, so just hang on to it for me, OK? Now, for *riding*," she said, hooking her arm through mine, "you won't want anything too fussy. And nothing light-coloured. On the other hand, you want to look good. I mean, who knows? This one could be The One. Leave it to me, I'll find you something!"

Nervously I said, "It's got to be in the sale."

"Yes, yes! Don't worry. How about this blue one? You could wear it with jeans, cos you'll have to wear jeans, unless you've got proper riding gear. Have you got proper riding gear?"

Meekly I shook my head. Katie, like Keri, is a bit of

40

a bossyboots, but sometimes I think it is good for me to be bossed, as left to myself I am not very organised.

When I got home (with my new blue top) I asked Mum if it would be OK for me to go riding with Keri on Tuesday afternoon. She said of course it would. "So long as they give you a hard hat to wear. You're not to go if they don't give you a hat! You're to promise me."

I promised, and Mum said, "In that case, no problem!" But then, thinking it would be a weight off her mind, I made the mistake of telling her that Keri was going to pay. Omigod! You'd have thought I'd said I was going to sell my body, or something.

Rather sharply, Mum said, "What do you mean, Keri is going to pay?"

"She's going to treat me."

"Oh, no!" said Mum. "No way!"

I know that secretly Mum doesn't really approve of Keri. She thinks she is spoilt and arrogant, which I suppose she probably is, but she is also very generous. She has always been willing to share. Mum just has this thing about not accepting charity. She said, very firmly, that she and Dad would pay and she didn't want any argument.

"We may not be rolling in money, but I think we can rake up enough for you to go riding. Just this once," she added, before I could start getting any ideas.

"Maybe for my birthday?" I said. "If I really like it? Cos you know it's something I've always wanted to do!"

"Let's wait and see," said Mum. "See how you get on."

That sounded hopeful!

Frizz rang later, and I told her that I'd decided to go riding after all.

"Not so much to meet this boy," I said. "Just cos it's something I've always, always wanted to do. I don't really care about meeting boys." Liar, liar, pants on fire! But it was true that horse riding *was* something I'd always wanted to do. "I mean, he might be OK," I said, "or then again he might not. Either way, it doesn't really bother me."

"In that case you can come with us tomorrow," said Frizz.

I said, "Come where? Where are you going?"

Excitedly, Frizz told me that a new veggie bar had opened down the market. "We're going to go and check it out!"

Keri would have rolled her eyes, for sure, but these things are important to Frizz and Darren. They are both going to be chefs when they leave school. Veggie is specially important to Frizz as she is going to be what she calls a *cordon vert* chef, meaning she is going to specialise in vegetarian food.

"We're going to go and sample the menu," she said. "See if we can pick up any new ideas."

"What, just you and Darren?"

"No! We've asked Kevin to come...specially! So's you don't feel like you're the odd one out, with me and Darren talking food all the time. We're meeting in the Town Hall Gardens, five o'clock. Is that all right?"

What could I say? When Frizz was trying so hard? I told her that I would be there. Kevin on Monday, Stuart on Tuesday... I was playing the field!

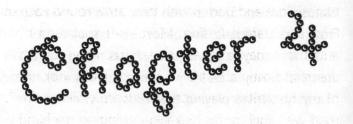

Chapter 4

Mum thought it was lovely that I was going out with Frizz and Darren.

"You and Dawn used to be so close, you used to do everything together."

"Mum, that was when we were *little*," I said. Not that me and Frizz weren't still good friends, but she had Darren, now. It was she and Darren who did things together.

"Well, I still think it's nice," said Mum. "I know you're more excited about going riding, but I have a very soft spot for Dawn."

What she meant was that she trusted Frizz, whereas she'd never really trusted Keri, not even when we were in primary school. She used to say that Keri was like ten going on twenty.

"And Darren," she said, "he's such a nice young lad. It's so sweet to see the two of them together!"

I said, "Yeah, yeah, yeah," while secretly thinking,

yuck, yuck, yuck! I always thought yuck when Mum started on about young love. Frizz and Darren holding hands, Frizz and Darren with their arms round each other, Frizz and Darren *kissing*. Maybe – I supposed I had to admit it – maybe I was just jealous. After all, I had my dreams; mostly about Lily's Joel, or Joel's lookalike. One of my favourites was where we were walking down the road with Joel (or his lookalike) swinging my hand when suddenly we'd stop, in full view of everyone, and go into a clinch. Some of the neighbours would catch sight of us and report back to Mum, saying how sweet it was. *That* was what I was jealous of! I wasn't jealous of Frizz having Darren, I was jealous of Mum thinking they looked sweet.

Defiantly, as I prepared to set out, I said, "I'm not bothering to get dressed up. It's only a snack bar type of place."

"That's all right," said Mum. "You look perfectly respectable."

I had in fact spent ages deciding what to wear; I always do. I'm one of those people, whatever I settle for, it always turns out to be wrong. But I was only meeting Frizz and Darren! Frizz has never had any dress sense, and Darren is quite a lumping sort of boy. On the other hand, there was the unknown Kevin. He *might* turn out to be The One…but I didn't really think so. Not if he was a mate of Darren's. But then again, I once read this article in a magazine which said you should always be prepared.

Even if Kevin wasn't The One, who knew what gorgeous boy I might bump into as I got on the bus? I might fall *off* the bus, straight into his arms. A fight might break out on the top deck and the gorgeous boy might save me! Anything could happen. You had to be prepared…

"Have fun," said Mum.

"Why, where's she off to?" said Craig as he came into the kitchen.

"Going on a date," I said, at the same time as Mum said, "She's meeting Dawn."

Craig sniggered. "Some date!"

I said, "Frizz isn't the date, you blithering moron!"

"It's a friend of Darren's," said Mum.

Craig looked at me and rolled his eyes. I felt like walloping him. Just because Darren is a bit – well! A bit of a pudding, really and truly. Still there wasn't any call for Craig to go pulling faces.

"Sounds like it's gonna be a wild night," he said.

It wasn't, of course; I hadn't expected it to be. I'm not quite sure what I was expecting. But I have to be honest and confess my heart did rather sink when I turned in to the Town Hall Gardens to see Frizz and Darren and this really goofy-looking boy waiting for me. I forced my lips into a smile. It is wrong – wrong, wrong, wrong! – to judge people solely on their appearance. I knew better than that. The poor boy couldn't help having teeth like a horse and no chin and big dangling hands. If I could just manage to take no notice I would probably find he was actually a really bright, funny, warm-hearted sort of person.

I widened my smile into a big beam as I approached. Frizz said, "Polly! This is Kevin. Kev, this is my friend Polly."

I said, "Hi."

Kevin grinned; a big toothy grin. "Going veggie tonight," he said.

"Don't worry," said Frizz. "It won't kill you."

"Won't kill any animals, either," I said.

"That's right." He nodded. "Won't kill animals." Then he grinned again. "Might have to eat a few when I get back home, though!"

"Shut up," said Frizz, "and don't be disgusting. Polly's into animals. She's got a dog, haven't you?"

I said, "Yes," but didn't feel inspired to say any more. Kevin was still grinning.

"They eat dogs," he said, "in Korea. Breed 'em special. Keep 'em in cages. People go and buy dog same as over here they buy bacon. It's—"

I stuffed my fingers into my ears.

Frizz yelled, "*Kevin!*" and thumped him.

"It's just his sense of humour," said Darren.

Frizz whispered, "He's a bit shy."

He didn't seem very shy to me. He said that he was sorry, but I didn't really think he was; he didn't sound very

47

sorry. With this sly smile he informed me that "Vegetables have feelings too, you know. They scream, vegetables do, when you chop 'em up."

"First I heard," said Frizz.

"That's cos it's ultrasonic. Like bats." Kevin made a high squealing noise.

Darren shoved at him. "What d'you know?"

"Not a lot." Kevin grinned again, showing his big horsey teeth. "Just thought I'd get a bit of conversation going."

I knew then, if I hadn't known before, that Kevin was definitely not The One. He wasn't bright and he wasn't funny, and if he really thought it was amusing to eat dogs then he wasn't warm-hearted, either. I decided that I loathed and despised him. Apart from anything else, he was a bore. He kept trying to tell me these really stupid jokes, like really, *really* stupid.

"What d'you get if you cross a cat with a ball of wool? *Mittens!* What d'you call an interfering pig? *A nosy porker!* See, I'm telling you animal jokes cos you like animals."

I absolutely refused to laugh, I refused even to smile, but it didn't stop him. He just went on and on.

"What's big and green and has a trunk? *An unripe elephant!*"

Coldly, I said, "That is pathetic."

It still didn't stop him. If he hadn't been so loathsome about people eating dogs I might have excused him. I might have thought he was nervous and telling jokes

48

was his way of covering up, and then maybe I might have forced myself to at least twitch my lips, just to be polite; but I kept thinking of those poor dogs kept in cages, waiting to end up on someone's plate, and I felt a sort of mad despair come over me and wanted to smash things. I thought if he didn't stop soon I would pick up a glass of water and throw it at him.

My first attempt at playing the field had failed miserably. I didn't even bump into a gorgeous boy on the bus. I didn't even *see* a gorgeous boy on the bus. I was just relieved, when I finally got home, that Craig wasn't there. It meant that when Mum asked me if I'd had a good time I could truthfully say, no. Of course, she wanted to know why, and so I poured it all out, about the dogs, and the stupid jokes, and the big horsey teeth. Mum said, "Oh, poor lad, he was probably just trying to impress you."

"Think how you'd feel," added Dad, "if you had big horsey teeth. Boys can be just as sensitive as girls, you know."

I snapped, "I don't think it's very sensitive when you know someone's got a dog and you go and tell them that in Korea they keep them in cages and eat them!" I snatched up Bundle and buried my face in his fur. "I'm going to bed," I said.

"But it's only half-past eight," said Mum.

I said, "I don't care! I'm going to go and read my book

49

and pretend none of it ever happened. And I'm taking Bundle with me!"

Just let Mum complain about dogs on the bed, shedding fur and making the sheets dirty. But she didn't say a thing. Just exchanged glances with Dad and silently shook her head. I guess she felt I'd had enough to put up with for one evening.

The only reason I didn't spend for ever choosing what to wear next day was that I already knew: my blue top with my best pair of trainers and the jeans I'd got for Christmas, the ones with the embroidery. I'd stayed awake half the night, mentally trying them on. Mum seemed to think the jeans were a mistake.

"They're a bit smart, aren't they?" she said. "Just for going riding?"

I thought, *Mum, that's the whole point!* I didn't want to look a mess.

"Haven't you got something older you could put on? What about those trousers you wore the other day for walking Bundle?"

Disgusting, shabby, washed-out, flappy things that made my bum look like some kind of huge inflatable beach ball. No, thank you!

"Well, it's up to you," said Mum, "but I think you'll be sorry."

The minute I saw Keri, all done up in proper riding trousers and long boots, I knew that for once Mum was wrong. If I'd worn the washed-out flappy things I would just have died with shame.

"Don't forget," called Mum, as we left, "wear a hat!"

"Fuss, fuss, fuss," I said.

"No, but she's right," said Keri, "you'll have to wear one. It's a safety thing."

"I'm not going to *fall off*," I said, "am I?"

"At the walk?" Keri giggled. "It has been known! First day he went out, Stuart dived headfirst into a bed of nettles when his horse wasn't even *moving*. But don't worry," she added, "we'll find something really comfortable for you. Dapple, maybe. Sitting on her's like sitting in an armchair. No need to panic!"

"I'm not," I said.

"Really?" She looked at me, like she was not sure whether to believe me. I was a bit surprised myself, as by nature I am what Mum calls a worry guts. But however hard I rummaged about inside my head, searching for secret fears, I couldn't find any. I was so eager to get to the stables and see the horses that even the thought of diving headfirst into beds of nettles didn't bother me. I'd only asked about falling off cos I was anxious not to look stupid in front of Stuart. But now I knew he'd managed to come off when his horse wasn't even moving I felt quite bold, and swore to myself that I would stick to the saddle like glue.

"I won't embarrass you," I promised Keri.

"So long as you don't *scream*," she said. "There was

a girl last week, she started shrieking every time we just broke into a trot."

"I won't scream," I told her.

"It makes you look like such a tit," said Keri.

Well! I didn't want to look like a tit, especially when we arrived at the stables and I was introduced to Jake. Omigod, he was practically a clone of Joel! Dark and gypsyish, with curly black hair.

"*Mine,*" mouthed Keri, behind his back. And then she gave a wicked grin, cos she knew she was quite safe. I wasn't any competition. "Look, here's Stuart. Not bad, eh?"

I spun round, expecting the worst. I knew Keri meant well, but I also know that I am not beautiful, or even specially pretty, in spite of Dad once telling me that I had a nice little face. Nobody was going to introduce me to a clone of Joel.

He wasn't a clone; nothing like. But at least he didn't have huge horsey teeth or big dangling hands. And when he said hello, I found myself thinking that I might, maybe, almost be able to fancy him. He had these very pale blue eyes, and a noble sort of nose, by which I mean it wasn't just a blob. He *could* turn out to be The One. I was just so thankful I hadn't followed Mum's advice about the old flappy trousers!

"OK," said Keri. "So who's Polly going to have? I thought maybe Dapple?"

Jake shook his head. "Can't have Dapple, she's already been on a three-hour hack. How about Jet?"

"Jet?" Keri looked at him; she seemed a bit doubtful.

"She's small enough for him," said Jake.

"I know, but...*Jet*?"

"He needs the exercise. He'll be all right."

"Well, if you're sure."

"Don't worry about me!" I cried. "I'll be OK!"

"Course you will," said Joel. "Not like we're going to do anything mad."

"What about my one?" Stuart sounded anxious. "Who am I having?"

Jake grinned. "Don't panic, we've got the sofa-bed for you!"

"Nobody," said Keri, "*ever* parted company with the sofa-bed. Come on!" She set off across the yard. "Let's get them out. You two wait here."

"Is that what you wanted?" I said to Stuart. "The sofa-bed horse?" I honestly thought, just for a moment, that it might be some kind of special breed.

"Well, if they'd wanted me to ride the maniac they put me on last week," said Stuart, "I'd have gone straight back home. They gave me this dreadful thing called Henry...Hooray Henry. That's his nickname. Gets the wind in his tail, you can't stop him."

I said, "Wow."

"It was terrifying. I've only had a few lessons!"

"I've never had any," I said.

"Stick with me," said Stuart. "You'll be all right with me. I've been on Delilah before. She never takes off."

"What about Jet?"

"Jet..." He frowned. "He's just a pony. Well, they're all ponies, really. But Jet's tiny."

"Does he ever take off?"

"Never been on him. He's too small for me."

"But if he's small, he's probably quite safe?"

Stuart's eyes slid away. "Guess he must be or they wouldn't put you on him."

"But they put you on Henry."

"Mrs Barnard, that was."

"Who's Mrs Barnard?"

"Woman that owns the stables. Got a face like a bucket."

I giggled at that.

"Wasn't funny," said Stuart. "She puts me on this mad horse then keeps yelling at me to keep his head up. How could I keep his head up? He needs an experienced rider. I've only had a few lessons."

I began to wonder why he was having lessons at all, since he didn't seem to enjoy them very much. Glumly, as if reading my mind, he said, "I thought it'd be fun. I thought I'd meet girls."

"And haven't you?" I said.

"Not the sort anyone'd want to go out with. All

they can think about is horses."

"Keri doesn't only think about horses," I said.

He turned a bit pink when I said that. "Yeah, well, Keri," he mumbled. "She's got this thing going with Jake."

"Is Jake in charge?" I said.

"Only when Bucket Face isn't here. He's far too young," said Stuart. "It's ridiculous!"

Jake didn't seem too young to me; I thought he was probably about seventeen. Practically grown up, and way too old for Keri. She was still only thirteen, however much she liked to play at being so sophisticated.

"Here you go." She and Jake were coming across the yard leading our two horses. Ponies. I must get it right! Delilah, otherwise known as the sofa-bed, was big and sandy-coloured, with a cream mane. She looked kind, and gentle. Jet hardly came up to her shoulder. He was black all over, and a bit shaggy. I had to suppress an urge to go and cuddle him.

"Oh," I said, "he's so cute!"

"He can be," said Keri. "You just have to watch him, cos he's got a mind of his own. Here!" She handed me a hat. "Put this on, otherwise we'll be breaking the law. Now, I'm going to give you a quick lesson before we actually go out. OK?"

I nodded, beaming. I couldn't wait to get into the saddle! Keri showed me how to hold the reins, how to sit, told me to keep my heels *down* and my back *straight*, gave me a short walk round the yard and we were off, single file up the lane. Jake took the lead, me following, then Stuart, and Keri bringing up the rear. Every now and again she would yell things like, "Keep those heels down! Tuck those elbows in!" I thought she must be yelling at me until in tones of exasperation she shrieked, "Stuart, how many more times?" and I heard Stuart muttering to himself. As we left the lane and came out on to a flat stretch of grass, Keri trotted past us.

"Me and Jake are going to go for a bit of a canter. You two just walk, OK? We'll wait for you at the far end."

"They shouldn't do that," said Stuart. "They're meant to be keeping an eye on us. We shouldn't be left on our own. You'd better rein that horse in," he added.

I said, "I'm trying!" I was tugging like mad on the reins, but Jet was tugging, too.

"He'll break away with you, then we'll both be in trouble."

I had a feeling I was already in trouble. Jet was tossing his head up and down and bucking, like he was trying to get rid of me.

"For God's sake," screeched Stuart, "control him, can't you?"

"I can't," I panted. In the tugging competition, Jet was definitely winning.

"Shorten the reins! Haul him in! You'll have us both off!"

56

Even as I was struggling, I felt a moment's irritation. It wasn't the least bit of good yelling at me. I'd never been on a horse before in my life!

Jet obviously sensed it; he knew I hadn't a clue. Triumphantly, he threw up his head, almost catapulting me out of the saddle. Next minute he was off, galloping flat-out in pursuit of the others, with me bobbing and bouncing on top of him. As he lit out, I heard a strangulated cry coming from somewhere behind me, but I didn't dare turn my head to look. I seemed to be slipping sideways. I *was* slipping sideways! For a moment, I nearly panicked. It was a great temptation to let go of the reins and grab hold of Jet's mane, but I just managed to stop myself. I thought, *heels down, elbows in*, and I gripped like crazy with my knees and hung on for dear life as the world flashed past me, trees on one side, road on the other.

Then, quite suddenly, I got the rhythm! Instead of bouncing and slipping it was like back and forth, to and fro, in time to the beat of the horse's legs. I could have gone on for ever! Just at the very last minute, as Jet caught up with the others and skidded, snorting, to a halt, I nearly came unseated, but Jake said "Whoa!" and caught at the reins and I managed to hold on.

"Sorry about that," said Jake. "Dunno what came over him."

I laughed, exultantly. "He wanted to catch up with you!"

"And you stayed on." Keri was looking at me like I was one of the Seven Wonders of the World. "You sure you haven't had lessons before?"

"Never even been on a horse," I said proudly.

"Obviously a natural," said Jake.

Keri nodded slowly. "I kept expecting you to bale out...I never thought you'd make it."

"I nearly didn't," I said. "I nearly slipped over the side."

"But you managed not to," said Keri. "You hung on in there!"

For the first time ever – ever, *ever* – there was a note of respect in her voice. She hadn't respected me when I'd got a scholarship to the High School. She hadn't respected me when I'd won a prize for writing an essay, or got a poem in the school magazine. But by staying in the saddle, and what was more, *not screaming*, I'd finally succeeded in impressing her. It's not that I really care two straws what Keri thinks of me – well, one straw, perhaps. *Half* a straw – but I have to admit, it did make me feel good!

"What's happened to the nerd?" said Jake.

We all turned, and shaded our eyes against the sun. In the distance we saw a lone figure, leading a horse. Jake rolled his eyes.

"I guess we'd better go back and get him. And, you," he wagged a finger at me, mock reproving. "No racing, this time!"

"What happened?" cried Keri, as we drew near. "Did you come off?"

"I *got* off," said Stuart.

"What for?"

"Because she was galloping! Totally irresponsible," he grumbled.

"Can't blame Polly," said Jake. "It's my fault, if anyone's. I honestly never thought Jet would take off like that."

"Delilah wouldn't have," said Keri. "If you'd just stayed put—"

"No, *thank* you." Stuart gave a sniff as he hauled himself back in the saddle. "I didn't come out to get my neck broken."

"Don't know why he comes out at all," said Keri, later, as we waited for her mum to pick us up from the stables.

"He wants to meet girls," I said.

"Well! He's met one. What d'you reckon?"

"He's a bit wimpy," I said.

"Yeah." Keri sighed. "Sorry about that. Guess it hasn't really worked out. Don't worry! I'll keep looking."

It hadn't worked out with Kevin, and it hadn't worked out with Stuart. But I'd been for a gallop and I'd stayed on! And now I wanted more than anything to do it again. Except...all I could think was, "What fun it would be if I could do it with Rees!"

I'd always bemoaned the fact that Rees and I had never gone anywhere or done anything except when he'd suggested it, which was mainly because I had never had any ideas of my own. Now I had, and it was all too late…

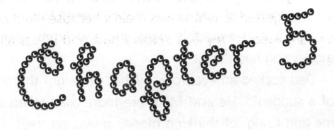

Chapter 5

Next morning, as he was about to leave for work, Dad said, "I hear you were triumphant yesterday."

For just a moment I honestly didn't know what he was talking about. I'd woken up feeling really miserable, thinking about Rees. Wishing we were still together. Missing him *so much*. All the exhilaration of my mad gallop had faded into almost nothing.

"You went riding?" prompted Dad.

"Oh! Yes. Riding! It was fun."

"Your mum and I have been discussing whether we could afford to let you have lessons. I know you've always wanted them. How about it? Good idea?"

I said, "Crumbs!" Thinking even as I said it that I sounded like something out of Enid Blyton.

"Well?" Dad held out his arms. "Don't I get a thank you?"

Awkwardly, I went on tiptoe and planted a kiss on

his cheek. When have I ever been awkward with Dad?

"Thank you," I whispered.

"That the best you can manage?" joked Dad.

"It's just...I wouldn't want you and Mum spending money you hadn't got!"

Dad cocked an eyebrow. "What's brought this on, all of a sudden?" He and Mum are more used to accusing me and Craig, of thinking money grows on trees. I told Dad that it worried me he might go bankrupt. But he laughed at that and said he wasn't going to go bankrupt just yet, and until he did he reckoned I should have my riding lessons.

"You deserve them, you've waited long enough. Arrange it with your mum."

It was Mum who brought the subject up, rather than me. "When would be a good time for you to go?" she said. "Saturday morning? Saturday afternoon?"

Saturday afternoons were when me and Rees used to do things. Go for a walk, take the dogs to classes. Watch a football match. Play chess. Not that I had ever properly learned to do more than just move a few pawns about. Rees was into chess in a big way. He had done his best to teach me, but I had just been too stupid. I hadn't even tried!

"What do you think?" said Mum. "Saturday afternoon?"

I told her that I would consult Keri and went up to

62

my room to call her on my mobile, but even as I brought up her number, I hesitated. I *did* want to go riding, but I didn't want to go with that wimpy Stuart. I wanted to go with Rees! It would be such fun, the two of us. Rees wasn't a wimp. *He* wouldn't have to ride on a sofa-bed horse.

I sat cross-legged on the floor, clasping my mobile, my thumb hovering over the buttons. Keri had told me not to worry, she would keep looking; but how many boys did you have to meet before you found the right one? Keri had met simply loads, she had been *out* with simply loads, and she still hadn't found the right one. It didn't seem to bother her, but I knew that it would bother me. I am not very good with new people; I can never think what to say or how to behave.

That was why it had been so comfortable, being with Rees. How could I ever have thought he was boring? Kevin was boring! Kevin was a moron, going on about people eating dogs and telling all those stupid jokes. You couldn't have an intelligent conversation with someone like that. Me and Rees had had conversations all the time. Long ones, about anything and everything. I'd never had any trouble thinking what to say or how to behave when I'd been with Rees. I'd just been able to relax and be me.

There and then I came to a decision: I wasn't going to play the field! I didn't want Keri to keep looking. Far better if I simply got on with my life and stopped worrying. It wasn't like I was the only person without a boyfriend. There was Lily, for a start, and Chloe. I would ring one of them! Maybe I would ring both; we could go out as a threesome. Who needed boys?

I decided that I would try Lily first, but just as I was about to dial her number the phone started warbling of its own accord. I know it's pathetic, but my first thought was, "Rees!" Of course it wasn't him. It was Chloe, all fizzing and bubbling.

"Got something to tell you!"

"Ooh," I said, trying my best to sound eager. "Something exciting?"

She giggled. "You'll never guess what!"

"What?"

"Remember that boy?"

"Which boy?"

"Chad. The one that was going to ring me and never did?"

"Oh. Yeah," I said. "Chad."

"Well, he rang me!"

"After all this time?"

"He's been sick," said Chloe. "He's had glandular fever!"

I didn't know what to say to that. Fortunately I didn't have to say anything as Chloe went merrily burbling on.

"It just goes to show, you never can tell. I nearly died when I heard his voice! He was like, I'm really sorry

I didn't call, you must have given up on me, and I'm like no, no, that's all right, cos you know, what else could I say? I didn't want him thinking I'd been waiting by the phone, but I didn't want him thinking I wasn't interested any more, cos I mean if he was ringing to say let's get together, which he *was*—" Chloe's voice shrieked at about a thousand decibels in my ear. "Well, I mean, when he said he'd been sick I just felt so awful, cos I really honestly thought he'd been having me on, you know?"

"Yes," I said. "I know." We'd been over it a hundred times.

"So, anyway—" She went into peals of happy laughter. "We're seeing each other this afternoon!"

I had to say that I was pleased for her; it would have been horridly mean not to. And I *was* pleased. I had to be pleased! I hated all these nasty little prickles of jealousy that were running about all over me. How could I be jealous of Chloe, who had waited so long and so patiently? I couldn't. I wasn't! And anyway, I still had Lily. I felt very close to Lily since she'd been so sympathetic about Rees. Far more so than either Keri or Frizz.

I transferred myself from the floor to the bed and dialled Lily's number. Her dancing school was on half term, same as us, and I knew she and Joel didn't usually see each other out of term time. Lily would be glad to have some company!

"Hi," I said, when she answered the phone. "I'm going

into town to find a book on horse riding. Want to come and help me?"

"I don't know anything about horse riding," said Lily.

"Well, you could look for a book on ballet."

"I've already got books on ballet!"

"Yes, but think of all the ones you *haven't* got. You can never have too many," I said.

"I know," said Lily, "but I haven't any money."

"That's all right, you can look at the pictures. You might find something about that prima ballerina person you went to see."

"Mm." There was a pause, as Lily seemed to consider the matter. "Are you going right now? If you're going right now, I'll come."

I said, "OK, you're on! See you in half an hour, usual place."

I told Mum I was going to meet Lily and look for a book on horse riding.

"Good idea," said Mum, "but don't you want something to eat before you go?"

"Can't," I said, "I promised Lily I'd leave straight away."

Lily was waiting for me in our usual spot, at the top of the escalator by some potted plants. She was wearing a bright red, sleeveless top, and an extremely short black skirt. She looked even tinier and daintier than ever.

"Is that new?" I said, pointing to the top.

Lily nodded, and blushed. I couldn't imagine what she was blushing for, but she had this air of suppressed excitement, like she was waiting for something to happen. I led the way into the bookshop and asked where the horse books were kept. Lily stuck with me.

"Don't you want to look at the ballet stuff?" I said.

She giggled and said no, she'd help me look at horse books. I wondered what she was giggling for. She was in a very strange mood!

I didn't buy anything in the end as I couldn't really afford it, and anyway it had mostly just been an excuse for meeting Lily. I'd hoped that maybe we could mooch around together for the rest of the afternoon, but Lily, blushing again, said she had something to do at two o'clock.

I tried not to let my disappointment show. "Something nice?" I said.

Her blush grew deeper.

"What?" We were sitting on the edge of one of the fountains, eating crisps. Well, I was eating crisps, Lily was just munching the odd one now and again. "What are you doing?"

"Meeting someone." She mumbled it so low I almost didn't hear.

I said, "*Meeting* someone? What, here?"

"Down by the clock."

We both turned to gaze at the clock, which bonged out the hours on the floor below. I waited for Lily to tell me who it was she was meeting. It couldn't be Joel; she'd have said if it were Joel.

"Someone from your dance school?" I said.

Lily shook her head. Oh, she can be so maddening when she clams up! She has always had this tendency to be secretive.

"It's a boy," I said, "isn't it?"

Her cheeks fired up, and I knew that I had guessed correctly.

"Well, go on, go on!" I said. "Tell me!"

But Lily just swung her legs and went on gazing fixedly at the clock.

"Is he a dancer?"

Lily said no, he was just an ordinary boy.

"So where did you meet him?"

Lily never goes anywhere or does anything unless it's connected with dancing. But it seemed this time she had. She told me that they had met at a youth club attached to the local church, St Joseph's, just down the road from where she lives.

"But you don't go to church!" I said.

"You don't have to," said Lily. "It's open to everyone… You could come, if you wanted."

I could go riding, I could go to Lily's youth club. But not on my own! Oh, why hadn't I thought of these things before?

"It's really good fun," said Lily. "Much better than

I thought it would be."

"Did you go there to meet boys?" I said.

"No! It was my mum, she was worried I was getting narrow-minded, just thinking about ballet all the time."

"Well, you probably were," I agreed. But that was Lily. She'd been obsessed by ballet ever since I could remember, even at primary school. I liked her that way.

"Mum's always said I should get some other interests going, in case I don't make it as a dancer."

Lily not make it as a dancer? I couldn't believe I was hearing this!

"Don't worry," said Lily, "I'm going to make it all right! But I didn't think there was any harm just giving it a go. Just to keep Mum happy, really."

So to keep her mum happy she'd gone to the youth club with a girl who lived over the road, and that was where she had met this ordinary boy. This boy that wasn't a dancer.

"He's never even seen a ballet!" gurgled Lily.

"So what do you talk about?" I said. I couldn't imagine Lily talking about anything that wasn't to do with ballet. Ballet was all she knew! "I mean…what do you have in common?"

"He's a boy!" said Lily, and gave a squawk of laughter, like him being a boy was enough in itself.

"What sort of things do you do?"

"Join in stuff at the Club… Oh, and tonight we're

69

going to the Music Festival. Festival-in-the-Park?"

I knew about the Festival. I'd probably have been going there with Rees if we hadn't broken up.

"Want to come with us?" said Lily.

I muttered that I didn't have anyone to go with.

"That's all right, Keri's coming."

"Yes, but she'll be with Jake."

"No, she's coming by herself. We're meeting her there."

"She's not going with Jake?"

"Jake's not her boyfriend," said Lily. "She just wishes he was! She's been after him for ages."

"So she'll be on her own?"

"I know, unheard of...Keri without a boyfriend!"

"Bet it doesn't take her long to find one. Bet you by the end of the evening she'll be hooked up!"

"Some poor unsuspecting soul..."

We both rolled our eyes.

"You going to come along, then?" said Lily.

"Aw, I dunno." I scrunched up my empty crisp packet. "I'm not feeling very sociable at the moment."

"That's cos you're missing Rees." Lily said it kindly. I would have liked to be able to toss my head and tell her that far from missing Rees I was glad we weren't together any more. But I couldn't. I'm not very good at keeping up a pretence, not even for the sake of my pride.

"I know it must be horrid," said Lily. "Makes you feel

70

like sort of…lost. I felt the same when I found out about Joel. I'd *so* thought of him as my boyfriend, and then suddenly knowing that he wouldn't ever be…well! It was like everything had just collapsed. Like the end of the world. You can't just hide yourself, away, though. You have to get out and meet people."

"I know," I said, "I know! Just don't rush me."

"You are coming on Saturday," said Lily, "aren't you?"

My heart sank. I'd been trying not to think about Saturday.

"You can't not come to Frizz's party!"

I mumbled, again, that I didn't have anyone to go with.

"You don't need anyone to go with! It's Frizz."

"It's still a party."

"But she's your best friend!"

And it was the first proper party she'd ever had. Frizz's mum and dad live in a flat over their shop. The shop is small, and the flat is even smaller, and they don't have very much money, I don't think. Less even than my mum and dad, so they couldn't do what some parents do and hire a hall. Frizz had once had a sort of birthday gig, back in Year 5, but there'd only been a handful of us there. She was really excited, this time, cos her mum had promised they'd clear one room entirely so she could invite as many people as she liked. Well, as many as could be squeezed in.

"Honestly, there'll be such a crush," I said, "she probably wouldn't miss me."

"*Pollee*!" Lily looked at me reprovingly. "Of course she'd miss you! And it won't be such a crush as all that. She's only invited us three, plus some of her friends from school."

"Plus boyfriends."

"Oh, well! Yes. Boyfriends," agreed Lily. "But she's got it all planned, she's going to use her bedroom, *and* the landing, *and*—"

"I know. She told me."

"*And* she's doing all the food!"

"I know."

"Her and Darren."

"I *know*!"

"So how can you possibly not come?"

I didn't like to admit that it was because Rees would be there. Frizz had sent him a separate invitation and I knew he'd be going because before we'd broken up we'd discussed what she would like as a present. I'd said, "Something to do with cookery," and Rees had looked appalled, like I'd suggested a peekaboo bra or frilly knickers, and said, "*Cookery?* You mean, a saucepan, or something?"

I'd giggled at that and said, "Or something!" Proudly he'd told me later that he'd got his mum to go shopping with him.

72

"We've got a sort of dish thing. One you can put in the oven. It's quite pretty, it's got flowers all over it. D'you think it's the sort of thing she'd like?"

I'd assured him that it was exactly the sort of thing Frizz would like. "A chef can never have too many dishes!" I'd thought it was really touching that he'd gone to so much trouble, even if it was probably his mum who'd done the actual choosing. Lots of boys wouldn't have bothered. They'd just have got a joke present, or something boring and predictable like shower gel.

"You've got to come," said Lily, "cos if you don't Frizz will be ever so disappointed." And then she turned bright crimson all over again and said, "Andrew's here, I've got to go. See you Saturday!"

I leaned over the rail, watching as Lily scudded down the escalator. I saw a boy, waiting by the clock. As Lily approached, he broke into a smile. The sun was shining on his hair, which was bright gold. He didn't look like a very ordinary sort of boy to me – he looked a bit Greek-god-like.

I watched as he and Lily walked off together. They were holding hands! How long had they known each other? It had been months before me and Rees had got to the hand-holding stage. Even months after, we still hadn't really got much further. Why had we been so *slow*?

I turned, and trailed off in Lily's wake, down the escalator. There didn't seem much point mooching round the shopping centre by myself. There didn't seem much point in anything, just at the moment.

Chapter 6

Later on at home, as we were about to sit down to tea, my phone rang. It was Frizz, wanting to know if I was going to the festival. I told her I didn't think so and she said that was a shame as she and Darren were going and Kevin might be joining them.

"Maybe he'd do for Keri," I said. "She's between boyfriends, if you can imagine it."

"Can't," said Frizz. "The mind boggles! You are coming on Saturday, aren't you?"

I made vague noises into the telephone.

"You'd better!" said Frizz. "There'll be trouble if you don't."

I couldn't help wondering if Lily had been talking to her. I thought, honestly! The things that go on behind one's back.

Mum wanted to know what it was that I wasn't going to. "It's not the music festival, is it? Because your dad and

I were thinking it might be fun to pop along, just for a couple of hours. Craig's going—"

"Not with you!" roared Craig.

"Well, no, of course not with us," agreed Mum. "I'm sure you wouldn't be seen dead with us! How about you, Polly? Fancy a night out?"

I let myself be talked into it; I don't know why. I spent the whole time in fear and trembling lest I bump into Rees. What would I say to him? What would he say to me? Would he even acknowledge me? He might cut me dead!

I didn't see Frizz and Darren – or Kevin, thank goodness – but I did catch a glimpse of Lily and Andrew, with Keri. Keri and Andrew were standing together, laughing at something. Well, Keri was laughing – the loud, shrieky laugh she does when she wants to impress. Andrew had this big daffy grin on his face. Lily seemed to be a bit out of it. I did hope Keri wasn't taking over; it's this habit she has. I don't think she means to, she just can't help it.

It wasn't till we were on the way out that I saw Rees. He was with his mum and dad, and fortunately I was able to scuttle through the gates before he could catch sight of me. My only small crumb of comfort, just the tiniest little one, was that at least he wasn't with a girl.

Thursday morning, I had to go to the dentist. Mum had made appointments for both me and Craig, and we both grumbled about it.

"Nice way to spend half term!" That was Craig, crossly slamming the car door shut as he huffed his way into the back. "There's nothing wrong with my teeth!"

"Nothing wrong with mine, either," I said. "Not," I added darkly, "until he's had a go...prodding, and poking, and drilling holes, and leaving me in agony!"

"If there's nothing wrong," said Mum, "he won't have to drill holes and leave you in agony. Craig, I wish you wouldn't slam the car door like that. It's not necessary."

"Nor's a visit to the dentist!" Craig was specially mad cos he was supposed to be going out with one of his mates and had had to cancel. Mum said it was his own fault for forgetting, but for once I felt sympathy for him. Who goes and arranges dentist's appointments during half term? Not that I, personally, had anything else to do, but going to the dentist isn't my idea of fun. Isn't anyone's, I shouldn't think. Mum told us not to be such a couple of wimps.

"If you didn't stuff yourselves with junk food, your teeth wouldn't rot and you'd have nothing to be scared of."

"I'm not scared," said Craig. "I'm just p—"

Mum said, "Craig!"

"What?"

"I've told you before...don't use that word."

"What word?"

"The word you were going to say."

Craig glowered mutinously. "How d'you know what I was going to say?"

"I read your mind," said Mum.

Craig subsided into a muttering sulk and I took the opportunity to point out to Mum that it was her job to oversee what we ate.

"You shouldn't let us stuff ourselves with junk food! It's very irresponsible. Anyway, last time I came I only had to have one tiny filling."

"So why are you making all this fuss?" said Mum.

It was just a matter of principle, really; I always make a fuss when I go to the dentist. I hate the way they wrap you up like a baby, with a plastic bib, and ferret about inside your mouth, and spray water all over you, and stuff your cheeks with cotton wool. I especially hate the way they talk at you while they're doing it, and you can't talk back because of having your mouth gagging open so you just have to make noises like some kind of animal.

Craig and I tossed a coin to see who'd go in first, and I won.

"OK," I said. "You go."

Craig looked surprised and pleased, and shot out of the waiting room before I could change my mind.

"Wouldn't you rather have gone first and got it over with?" said Mum.

I said, "No! While there's life, there's hope."

"Meaning what?"

Meaning that anything could happen: the dentist could have a funny turn and have to go home; the town could be hit by an earthquake; the building could catch fire. Anything!

Needless to say, none of the above took place. Craig came out looking sorry for himself – "Gave me the needle!" – and I went in. I paid the price for being a coward cos while I was sitting in the chair being poked and prodded, my phone rang, twice. If I'd gone in first I'd have been in the waiting room and could have answered it. I find it *so* frustrating, not being able to answer the phone! And I might just as well have gone first, cos there wasn't anything that needed doing. *I* didn't have to have the needle! As I reported triumphantly to Mum, "I told you there wasn't anything wrong."

Craig had gone off to meet his mate, so I couldn't crow over him. He's always making like he's so superior just because he's a boy, which he seems to think makes him higher up the evolutionary scale than mere girls. Some boys are like that; they just feel they have to be top dog. It was what was so civilised about Rees: he *never* wanted to be top dog, just equals.

I sighed. Mum said, "What now?"

I shook my head. "Nothing. I missed two telephone calls!"

The first was from Lily, who sounded breathless and

bothered. She said, "Polly, this is Lily," and then abruptly rang off, without leaving any message. The second was a text from Frizz saying, "Call me".

I couldn't call immediately cos Mum and me were going shopping, but I rang as soon as we got home.

"Oh, thank goodness!" said Frizz. "We've got to talk. It's about Lily!"

I said, "Lily? She rang me! She didn't leave any message."

"That's cos she tried you first and when you weren't there she rang me. She's in a right state. We've got to do something! Can I come over?"

Frizz arrived twenty minutes later. Mum said, "Hello, Dawn! Lovely to see you. I tried that recipe you gave me, by the way. The one for risotto? It went down a fair old treat!"

Normally it would have been all the invitation Frizz needed. Start her off on recipes and she never stops! Today she just said she was glad the risotto had worked, and followed me up the stairs. I knew, then, that this was serious – and I think I could already guess what it was about.

"It's her new boyfriend," I said, "isn't it?"

"It's *Keri*," said Frizz.

My heart plummeted. "Oh, no!" I said. "She didn't?"

"She did!"

"You mean—" I really didn't want to believe it. Not even *Keri*. I clasped my hands over my face. "Don't tell me!"

"Lily's dreadfully upset. She was in tears on the phone."

"Omigod, I saw them," I said. "Last night, at the Festival? I went, in the end, with Mum and Dad. I saw them in the distance."

"Me and Darren bumped into them. Keri was behaving *abominably*. Even Darren noticed."

"Oh, she really is the pits!" I said. "How could she do such a thing?" And to Lily, of all people. Poor Lily! She had already had her heart broken once.

"It is just so mean," said Frizz.

"She didn't actually, like...go off with him, or anything?"

"No, she just *swamped*. You know the way she does? But then at the end, Lily said, she insisted on walking back with them—"

"Back to Lily's? But that's like in totally the wrong direction!"

"Lily thinks she was hoping Andrew would drop her off, then turn round and take Keri all the way back to her place."

"But he didn't." That, at least, was some relief.

"Lily doesn't *think* he did. But he offered to take her to the bus stop and wait until her bus came."

"Lily should have gone with them! Then he could have walked her back again."

"I think by then," said Frizz, "she was too upset. Honestly, you should have seen them! Well, it was Keri, really. Andrew wasn't doing anything."

I said, "No, he was just behaving like some kind of hypnotised rabbit!" It's the effect Keri has on boys. Some boys. Obviously it hadn't worked with Jake, so she'd gone all out to try her witchy wiles on Andrew. And he fell for it! "God," I said, "what is the matter with boys?"

"You mean, what is the matter with Keri," said Frizz. "She's getting worse and worse. We've got to do something! We can't just let her get away with it."

"Don't see there's much we *can* do," I said.

"We could go and have a word with her. Let her know how we feel."

"Mm…" I was a bit doubtful, to tell the truth. I really couldn't imagine Keri caring one way or another about how me and Frizz might feel. She would most likely just laugh at us.

"We could at least give it a go," urged Frizz.

"I dunno." I still hesitated. A phrase kept running through my head: *all's fair in love and war.* You had to be prepared to put up a fight. I felt pretty sure Keri wouldn't sit back and do nothing if somebody dared steal one of her boyfriends. She would go charging into battle immediately! I am too much of a wimp, and would probably just sit at home and be self-pitying. Lily has never been a wimp, but in some ways, like when it came to boys, she was still incredibly naïve. How could she have let such a thing happen?

"Polly!" Frizz was looking at me reproachfully. "Lily's our friend!"

I thought, *so is Keri*. Supposed to be. But Keri could look after herself; Lily couldn't. And I really did owe her.

"OK," I said, "let's do it. D'you want to ring her, or d'you want me to?"

"I'll do it," said Frizz.

I am ashamed to admit that I felt quite relieved when she said that. Keri can be *so* withering, and I still wasn't sure what we were going to say to her. Frizz obviously had no such doubts.

"I just hope she's there," she said, "cos I'm all geared up. We need to tackle her while the iron is hot."

"Don't you mean strike?" I said.

"What?"

"*Strike* while the iron is hot."

Frizz glared at me, and I immediately shrivelled. There was Lily, desperately miserable, and all I could do was witter and nitpick.

"Sorry," I mumbled. "You're right, we need to do it *now*."

Frizz didn't need my encouragement, she was already rummaging in her bag for her mobile. I couldn't ever remember her taking charge like this. Back in primary school she would never have dared have a go at Keri. Now she couldn't wait; I was the one hanging back.

"Well," she said, "it's ringing. At least that means she's not having one of her endless conver— Keri! Yes. It's me. I'm with Polly. We want to talk to you...not on the phone! We need to come round... No! *Now*. Yes. Right away." She looked at me and pulled a face. I raised an eyebrow. "I can't tell you on the phone! We're going to come over. *OK?*"

It was obviously going to be OK whether Keri liked it or not. Trying to make up for my previous lack of enthusiasm, I said, "That told her!"

"She needs telling," said Frizz. "She needs a lot more than just telling. Come on! Let's go."

Mum seemed surprised when we clattered back downstairs and headed for the door.

"Off again already?"

"Just going round to Keri's," I said.

"So long as I know," said Mum.

As we got off the bus and pounded up the hill to Keri's place, I tried to rehearse with Frizz what we were going to say, but she is one of those people, when she sets her mind to something she can be really stubborn. She said she knew what she was going to say, she didn't need to rehearse. I protested that it would all come out as a jumble, but she said, "You can rehearse if you want. I'm going to be spontaneous."

She pronounced it *sponteneeus*, but I didn't say anything. It didn't seem quite the right moment. I decided that since it had been Frizz's idea I would let her do all the talking. I would just be there as back-up.

Keri must have guessed why we were coming, but she put on her usual show as she led the way upstairs.

"Hi, you guys! Surprise, surprise! Woss up?"

Frizz got launched immediately. "It's about Lily."

Keri said, "Oh?"

"She's very upset."

"About what?"

"The way you behaved with Andrew."

"The way I behaved with Andrew?" Keri gave a little laugh and settled on the window seat, carelessly swinging her legs. "I didn't behave any way with Andrew!"

"Yes, you did," said Frizz. "I was there. I saw you!"

"So what was I doing?"

"Flirting."

"Oh, for goodness' sake!" Keri rolled her eyes. "You call that flirting?"

Frizz said, "Yes, and so does Lily."

"Well, honey chile," Keri said in a silly exaggerated drawl, "If that's what you call flirtin', you ain't never seen flirtin', is all I can say!"

She was behaving exactly as I'd known she would.

Making fun. Turning the tables. But Frizz stood her ground. I don't think I've ever admired her so much.

"You were shrieking," she said. "You were showing off! You were making up to him."

Keri fluttered her eyelashes. "I was just being my own true self, honey chile."

"You got him to take you back to the bus stop," I said, feeling it was time I made a contribution.

Keri swung round. "So what?" Her tone was decidedly hostile.

"So…" Rather timidly, I waved a hand. Fortunately, Frizz jumped in.

"So why did you *need* to go back to the bus stop? You shouldn't have been there in the first place! Why didn't you catch a bus when you left the park and let Andrew and Lily go on by themselves?"

"We were *having* a good *time*," said Keri. "Right? We were enjoying ourselves!"

"Lily wasn't."

"How do you know?"

"Cos she rang me!"

"You really hurt her," I said. Frizz didn't seem to need my input but I couldn't just sit there and say nothing. "She was so happy! She was really looking forward to last night. You know Andrew's the only real boyfriend she's ever had. Why did you have to go and ruin things for her?"

Keri bit her lip. For the first time, she seemed slightly less sure of herself.

"You're supposed to be her friend," I said. "She trusted you!"

"I know." Keri drew her knees up to her chin and wrapped her arms round them. Suddenly, all her bluster had gone. She spoke in a whisper. "I didn't mean it to happen! I don't set out on purpose to do these things. It's like something just takes over...you know?" She looked at us, almost pleadingly.

"You're just making excuses," said Frizz. "Nobody *has* to behave that way."

Keri let her head droop down on to her knees. For a moment I almost felt sorry for her. Who would have thought Frizz could be so merciless? Not that Keri didn't deserve it, but I hated to see her looking all defeated and pathetic.

Trying to be helpful, I said, "The trouble is, she sees a boy and she just can't resist trying to get him."

"Especially if he belongs to someone else!" Frizz said.

I wasn't quite sure that that was fair, but Keri didn't say anything to defend herself and Frizz just went barrelling on.

"First she goes and steals them, then, as soon as she's got them she loses interest! I suppose that's what you'll do with Andrew?"

"No!" Keri shook her head, quite violently. "You've

87

got it wrong! I didn't steal Andrew, I just—"

"Flirted with him! You might as well admit it," said Frizz.

"All right! I flirted with him. Just a little. But we're not going out, or anything! It was only a game. From now on," said Keri, "I give you my word, I won't even *look* at him!"

"That's all very well," said Frizz, "but it's a bit late for Lily. You've already gone and spoilt everything for her."

"I haven't!" Keri said it earnestly. "It's not too late. I'll make it all right with Lily. I promise!"

"Don't see how you're going to do that."

"I'll ring her. I'll apologise! It'll all work out. She's the one he really fancies. It'll be OK!" Keri stopped, and took a breath. "Gee, I'm really glad we had this talk. You guys should have done it a lot sooner. It's made me see myself as I really am."

"Which is what?" I said politely.

Keri gave one of her swoops of laughter. "A total failure!"

Pardon me?

"Where boys are concerned." She became sober again. "It's true! I've never had a proper relationship. Not like you two. I really envy you!"

"I haven't got a proper relationship," I said. "I haven't got a relationship at all!"

"You did have. I feel so guilty about that," said Keri.

"If it hadn't been for me, you and Rees would still be together."

"Well...maybe," I said.

"You would! You were a perfect match. Boffins, the pair of you! And Frizz and Darren...made for each other! Honestly, I'm not so sure about Lily and Andrew. Lily and *Joel*...if only he wasn't gay. But someone that's not into ballet? I can't see that lasting."

"What does it matter?" said Frizz. "So long as they're happy *now*."

"They will be, they will be!"

"You totally promise?"

"Cross my heart and hope to die! Just leave it to me," said Keri. "I'll fix it."

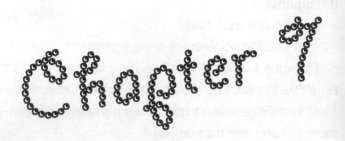

Chapter 7

"She'd better," said Frizz, as we walked back down the road.

"She will. I'm sure she will!" You can always rely on Keri to do what she said. It might not necessarily be something you *want* her to do, but you never have any doubt that she will go ahead and do it. She had been calling Lily even as we left. She wouldn't let us stay and listen, though; she said it would be too embarrassing.

"I'm going to *grovel*. Right?"

I couldn't help giggling at the thought of it. I would have loved to see Keri grovelling! Frizz wanted to know what was funny.

I said, "Keri, grovelling!" Frizz didn't even smile. She was obviously still cross.

"Oh, come on," I said, "give her a break! She did apologise."

"She still has to make things right. I'll believe it when it happens."

"Don't you trust her?"

"Do you?" said Frizz.

I hesitated. "Not always, not about everything. But this time I think I do. I think she really felt ashamed."

"Hm." Frizz stomped on for a bit in a kind of brooding silence. I reminded myself that she was the one who'd had to listen to Lily pouring her heart out. It must have been upsetting.

"Keri's not really a bad person," I pleaded. "Just a bit spoilt." I guess if your mum and dad have pots of money, plus you're an only child, it's difficult not to be. "She's just used to having everything she wants."

"Well, at least she feels guilty about you and Rees. That's something, I suppose."

I struggled for a moment with my conscience. I would have liked to hold Keri responsible, but I knew, really and truly, that I could only blame myself. I had gone out with another boy, just to see if another boy would be more exciting. OK, so Keri was the one who had egged me on, but that only meant I was pathetic and weak-willed and had no mind of my own.

"Would you go back with Rees," said Frizz, "if he asked you?"

"He won't."

"No, but if he did?"

"I told you, he won't!" Why would he ever even want to *see* me again, let alone go out with me? "I behaved every bit as badly as Keri," I said. She had hurt Lily, just as I had hurt Rees.

"Do you wish you hadn't done what you did?" said Frizz.

"Of course I do!" I screamed it at her. "Stop rubbing it in!"

"I'm not rubbing it in, I'm just trying to find out how you feel."

"I feel terrible, if you must know."

"Terrible for you, or terrible for Rees?"

"Both!" And then, irritably: "Why do you have to keep on?"

"See, when Darren kissed that stupid girl, I forgave him," said Frizz.

I looked at her uncertainly.

"Maybe Rees might forgive you."

I shook my head. "He won't ever forgive me."

"He might do. He might just be waiting for the opportunity. How do you know?"

"Cos I know!" I stuck my hand out. "This is my bus."

I was glad that Frizz was going on to Darren's, which meant the opposite direction. I couldn't take much more of her questioning!

"See you Saturday," called Frizz. "Yes?"

I flapped a hand. I really wasn't sure about Saturday.

The more I thought about it, the more I desperately didn't want to go. Rees would be there, and I wouldn't know what to say. I wouldn't know what to do! Would he even acknowledge me? And suppose he was there with another girl? I just couldn't bear it!

I woke up on Saturday morning with a huge lump of lead lying in the pit of my stomach. I knew how excited Frizz was, what with it being her first proper party; I knew how much she wanted us all to be there. But it was no use! I just couldn't. Apart from anything else, I really hate going to parties on my own. Everyone would turn up with a boyfriend, except me. Even Keri would find someone to go with. She might even go with Rees! She might think it was fair game, seeing as we'd split up. Rees didn't specially care for Keri, but it would be an excellent way of getting his own back. I really couldn't blame him; boys can be just as hurt as girls. But just cos I didn't blame him, it didn't mean I wanted to be there and watch!

"*So if you don't want to go,*" said a voice inside my head, "*don't go.*"

"*But Frizz!*" I thought.

"*Don't worry about Frizz,*" said the voice. "*Frizz has got Darren.*"

It was true. Frizz didn't need me! The leaden lump in my stomach instantly and miraculously disappeared. I gobbled down my breakfast and snatched Bundle's lead from its home in the vegetable rack.

"Oh," said Mum, sounding pleased, "are you taking him out?"

"Thought I might as well. Bundle, walkie!" Bundle shot out of his bed like a furry cannon ball. "It's not my turn," I told Craig, "but just for once I don't mind doing it."

Craig's eyes immediately narrowed. "What's your game?"

I said, "I'm doing you a favour!"

"Why?"

"Cos I feel like it."

"You're meeting someone," said Craig. "Who is it? Is it Knickers? Has he taken you back?"

I snapped, "None of your business! And don't call him Knickers." Just because his surname was Nicholson. *Such* an annoying habit!

"Call him what I like," said Craig. "What's it to you? Thought he'd given you the elbow."

I shouted, "You shut up!" and hurled a piece of toast at him. Craig ducked.

"'Bout time he did give you the elbow, way you treated him… I wouldn't take you back. I wouldn't take any girl back, treated me like that!"

The lead weight immediately plonked down again into my stomach. As I walked Bundle round the park I reminded myself that *Frizz had Darren*. What did it matter to her whether I went to her party or not? There'd be plenty of people without me! My mind was made up. Once and for all. I didn't want to go and I wasn't going to go, and that was all there was to it.

So why, why, why did everyone have to try and drag me there? They all rang up, one after another: Lily, Keri, Frizz. Lily was the first.

"Polly, you can't let Frizz down. You're her best friend!"

Then Keri. "I insist that you come! I've done my part. I rang Lily. We talked for simply ages… I grovelled like mad! Everything's all right again, she's coming with Andrew, they're back in lurv…the least you can do is be there to see it!"

Then Frizz. "*Please*, Polly! *Please* come. I can't have a party and you not be there!"

Even Mum had to weigh in.

"Isn't it about time you were getting into your finery?" she said, at half past six. "You know it takes you for ever! You're presumably not going like that? If you want me to give you a lift, you'd better get a move on, I'm due at work in an hour's time."

Mum was on late shift at the care home where she looks after old people. I told her that it was OK, I'd catch the bus.

"And how are you getting back? You'd better give your dad a ring."

I said, "Yes, all right."

"Unless someone offers you a lift. Keri's mum, maybe?

But still call Dad, just to let him know. Then he can settle down. Otherwise—" Mum stopped. "Are you listening?" she said.

I assured her that I was, but Mum is not easily taken in.

"Polly," she said, "you are *going*, aren't you?"

I shuffled uncomfortably.

"Oh, now, Polly, come on! This is Frizz," said Mum. "It's her big day! What's the problem? Is it because of Rees?"

"He's going to be there," I muttered.

"Well, you're bound to bump into him sooner or later. You both know the same people! You can't go on avoiding him indefinitely. And the longer you leave it," said Mum, "the more awkward it's going to be."

I heaved a sigh. I knew Mum was right.

"Be brave," she urged. "Get it over with! Go on, go and put your party clothes on and I'll give you a lift. Quick, quick! Twenty minutes."

I trailed upstairs and flung open the wardrobe door. I remembered how lovely Lily had looked, going off to meet Andrew in her little red top and her short skirt. I had a short skirt. I couldn't wear it very often because of Dad and his old-fashioned ideas. He would like it if I went round covered from head to foot like something out of Victorian times. But Dad wasn't back from work yet, and Craig was out, which meant I was safe from his infantile remarks.

I pirouetted in front of the mirror, in my short skirt and my new blue top. I wasn't anywhere near as pretty as Lily, and I certainly wasn't as tiny and dainty, but on the whole I liked what I saw. At any rate, I didn't find myself thinking, "Ugh, fat!" or "Yuck, bulges!" the way I sometimes do. Maybe I'd managed to lose a bit of flab, thanks to all the misery I'd endured. There had to be some compensations.

I did another twirl and went downstairs feeling a bit stronger. I had Frizz's present all ready and wrapped. I'd bought her a wooden spice rack, cos once when we were wandering through the kitchen department in one of the big stores in the shopping centre she'd picked one up and sighed longingly over it, saying, "That's quality, that is." To me a spice rack would be like the ultimate in boredom, but I think you have to buy people what they want and not what you would want for yourself.

Mum drove me into town and drew up opposite Frizz's place. The very minute we stopped, I began to get that leaden feeling in my stomach again.

"Well, off you go!" said Mum. "Don't forget your present."

I picked it up from the back seat and reluctantly opened the car door. My feet wiggled their way on to the pavement. Slowly I stood up, and slowly closed the door. Mum called after me: "Use the crossing!"

"Yes, Mum."

"Don't forget to give your dad a call when you're ready to go home."

"No, Mum."

"Enjoy yourself!"

"*Yes*, Mum."

Mum drove off, leaving me on my own. I walked to the crossing and pressed the button. A car came to a halt, but instead of walking across I just stood there, frozen. Over the road I could see that the shop was closed, but all the upstairs lights were on and I could hear faint sounds of music.

The car driver hooted his horn and waved at me impatiently. Like someone wading through treacle, I stepped out on to the crossing. The lights changed before I was even half way across, but my feet refused to hurry. It was only the memory of Frizz, pleading with me – *Please, Polly! Please come!* – that kept me moving. And then, suddenly, a car pulled up at the kerb just ahead of me and someone jumped out. It was Rees. It was Rees! Oh, God! What was I to do?

I cringed into the shadows, watching as he went up to the door. If he turned round, he would see me! I shrank back into the side alley between Frizz's shop and the Blue Moon café. My heart was pounding and thudding. I shouldn't ever have come. I had to get away! *Now*, before he saw me!

There was a bus trundling up the road. I couldn't make

out what number it was, but at least it was going in the right direction. Anything would do! Anything that got me away. I darted out of my hiding place – and bumped SLAP BANG! Right into Rees…

I went, "Oof!" Not actually meaning to, since "oof" is not really a word that you would choose to say. More like a sound that just splutters out of you.

"Polly!"

Rees stretched out a hand, then let it drop back again. We stood there, awkwardly staring at each other.

"I was just g—"

We both spoke at the same time. And both stopped.

"After you," said Rees.

I gulped. "I was just going to…" I gestured, feebly, as the bus rocked on its way without stopping.

"You were going to get the bus?" Rees seemed perplexed. Why would I be getting the bus when I was supposed to be going to Frizz's party?

"Think I've got the flu," I said.

"Really?"

No, not really! I'm just feeling ashamed and embarrassed and want to go home!

"You don't look like you've got the flu," said Rees. "You look really pretty!"

And then he blushed deep red, and I blushed, too, so now we were standing there like a couple of ripe tomatoes.

"I thought you'd have gone in," I said.

Rees looked uncomfortable. "Changed my mind," he muttered. "Decided not to go. Got cold feet, if you must know!"

Rees had got cold feet? Why would he have them? He wasn't the one that had done anything wrong!

"Didn't know what I'd say to you. Thought you wouldn't want to talk to me."

I swallowed. "I thought you wouldn't want to talk to me! I saw you there, and I – I got scared."

"Scared of me?"

"In case you hate me!"

"I don't hate you," said Rees.

"But I behaved so badly!"

"You said you were sorry."

"I am! I am sorry!"

"So'm I," said Rees. "I'm sorry we broke up. I'm sorry I didn't accept your apology, I'm sorry any of it ever happened! There's only one thing I'm not sorry about." He gave a little half grin. "I'm not sorry I changed my mind cos if I hadn't we wouldn't have bumped into each other!"

"I'd have got on the bus," I said, "and gone home."

"That's what I was going to do." He grinned again; a proper grin, this time. "They'd have been seriously mad at us," he said. "They've been ringing me up all day."

"Me too," I said.

"Frizz—" He stopped.

I said, "Frizz what?"

"She said—"

"What?"

"She said you'd—"

"*What*?"

"Doesn't matter." He shook his head, embarrassed. "She just said if I didn't come she wouldn't ever forgive me."

"She said that to me, too."

"Mind you, she wasn't the worst. Keri was the worst. She practically threatened me."

"She's like that," I said. I hesitated. "I thought maybe you might come with her."

"Me and Keri?"

"To get back at me," I muttered.

"I don't want to get back at you! I did," said Rees, "just at first. But then I thought about things, and I thought how we never seemed to do anything you wanted to do. It was always me."

"That's cos I could never think of anything. But just this week I thought of two things! I thought we could go horse riding? And join Lily's youth club, where she met Andrew? I mean…" I faltered. "They were things we could have done."

"Still could," said Rees. "If you wanted?"

"Oh, that would be such fun!" I said. "And then if you like we could go back to dog training, as well."

"You didn't enjoy dog training."

"I could give it another go."

"Nah! We've done that. Time for something new."

There was just a second's pause, and then it happened. All of a sudden, right there and then, standing on the pavement, we did something we had never done before. All it took was a quick glance, and next thing I knew we were kissing. Real, proper kissing like I'd begun to think I would never do with anybody. Like I *so* hadn't wanted to do with Rory! But now here I was, doing it with Rees, and might have gone on doing it for ever if someone hadn't thumped me on the shoulder and a familiar voice cried, "Go, boffs!"

Keri. Wouldn't you know it?

"That girl!" said Rees.

I don't think he really minded, though. Neither of us did. We were too happy to mind!

"So, you coming in, or what?" said Keri. "Oi, Boffins!" She thumped me again. "You coming?"

Rees looked at me. "What d'you reckon?"

I pulled a face. "I guess we'd better...she'll only nag at us."

"Dead right," said Keri. "What a way to behave!" She wagged a finger. "Ought to be ashamed of yourselves." And, "Hey, happy birthday!" she added, as Frizz appeared at the door. "See who I've brought with me!"

"Oh! You came, after all," said Frizz. "Both of you!"

Her face was one big happy beam. As we followed her and Keri up the narrow stairs, which I'd climbed so often before, I thought how lucky I was to have Frizz for a friend. And Lily! And Keri! We were the Gang of Four, and always would be.

"Way to go!" said Keri.

She always has to have the last word.

About the Author

Jean Ure had her first book published while she was still at school and immediately went rushing out into the world declaring that she was AN AUTHOR. But it was another few years before she had her second book published, and during that time she had to work at lots of different jobs to earn money. In the end she went to drama school to train as an actress. While she was there she met her husband and wrote another book. She has now written more than eighty books! She lives in Croydon with her husband and their family of seven rescued dogs and four rescued cats.

978 1 84616 963 2

£4.99

Despite being at her new school with
the uncool Jessamy James, Polly's making plenty
of new friends and earning herself a whole new
social life. But will new arrangements clash with
the gang of four's weekly Saturday meet-ups?

Will Polly be facing a friendship crisis? Or will the
girlfriends work it out?

978 1 84616 961 8

£4.99

Meet the girlfriends! Polly, Keri, Frizz and Lily.
They're the Gang of Four, and they're going to
stick together for ever and ever! Their bond of
friendship is severely tested, though, when they
discover that they are all going off to different
schools in the autumn. And poor Frizz is going to
be left with their archenemy, Jessamy James,
a show-off who wears pink knickers, which
they all know isn't cool!

978 1 84616 964 9

£4.99

The girlfriends are growing up and entering a whole new world, and boys are a major part of it. After their separate summer holidays, Polly is alarmed when her friends start showing an interest in boys, but is even more alarmed when boys start showing an interest in her! Reluctant to grow up, will Polly be left behind? Or will she realise that not all boys are what they seem...?

£4.99   978 1 84616 962 5

What's up with Frizz?

The gang of four are eager to talk about their talents, but Frizz is keeping quiet. Whatever happened to sharing everything and sticking together? Is Polly right in thinking she's just jealous, overshadowed by too much talent?

Or does Frizz have a secret of her own to share that will steal the spotlight?

978 1 40830 301 6

£4.99

The Gang of Four are growing up. It seems to Polly that they spend most of their spare time with their boyfriends, and even when they are together, all they do is talk about boys. Polly's not sure whether boys really *are* her. Wasn't it better when it was just the four girls and they could shop, gossip and not have to worry about boys all the time? Polly wonders whether she'll ever really understand what it's all about...

978 1 40830 302 3

£4.99

Polly is really looking forward to a trip to the
seaside with her best friends and their
boyfriends. It'll be brilliant, all eight of them
together! But then Polly's plans start to fall
apart as, one by one, her friends' relationships
hit trouble. Soon she finds herself stuck in the
middle, like some kind of agony aunt.
And when Polly finally gets her day by the sea,
will it turn out to be as much fun as she hopes –
or will it be a total disaster?

978 1 40830 303 0

£4.99

Polly's getting tired of doing the same things with her boyfriend, Rees, especially when his idea of fun is training their dogs together! Her friends' lives seem much more exciting.

So when another boy shows an interest, Polly decides she needs a change. But it's not just boys who can behave badly...